POPULAR PUBLICATIONS   FACSIMILE EDITIONS

Shock #2
(May 1948)

Shock was launched in 1948 by Popular Publications as a companion magazine to its primary detective pulps, *Dime Detective* and *Black Mask*, concentrating on weird-mystery stories. The second issue contains stories by Robert Turner, Bruce Cassiday, and John D. MacDonald.

Authors:

*Scott O'Hara, John Bender, Robert Turner, Henry Guth,
Bruce Cassiday, H. Hassell Gross, Wallace Umphrey,
John D. MacDonald*

Illustrators:

Frederick Blakeslee, Monroe Eisenberg

LADY MEETS LION AND THEN...

SALLY BRETT AND HER BROTHER JOE, ARE JUST TURNING HOMEWARD AFTER A DAY-LONG RIDE IN STATE CANYON FOREST WHEN...

THE DOGS HAVE TREED HIM! COME ALONG AND WATCH US GET HIM

YIP! YIP! YIP!

THAT'S THE END OF THAT CATTLE KILLER

NOW I'VE GOT TO WORK PAST...SION HIM AND HIKE TO CEDAR CITY BY DARK

THAT'S OUR BASE, TOO. SAY! YOU RIDE SIS'S HORSE AND WE'LL DOUBLE UP!

DINNER? THANKS, BUT I'D BETTER DRIVE TO THE RANCH. I'M HARDLY IN SHAPE TO APPEAR IN PUBLIC

DON'T WORRY, WE CAN CLEAN UP IN MY ROOM

LATER

RAZOR? SURE THING!

SHE'S A BEAUTIFUL GIRL

SAY, THIS BLADE'S SURE KEEN AND EASY-SHAVING... AND MY BEARD'S LIKE WIRE

TOUGH BEARD'S NO PROBLEM FOR THIN GILLETTES

I SURE WISH YOU'D ACCEPT, THERE'S PLENTY OF ROOM AT THE RANCH AND...

WE STILL HAVE A WEEK, SIS. HOW ABOUT IT?

I'D LOVE IT

HE'S SO HANDSOME!

YOU SKIM OFF TOUGH BEARD SLICK AS SILK... GET BETTER SHAVES AND MORE OF 'EM... WITH THIN GILLETTES. NO OTHER LOW-PRICED BLADE COMPARES WITH 'EM FOR KEENNESS AND LONG LIFE. THIN GILLETTES FIT YOUR RAZOR EXACTLY, TOO... NEVER SCRAPE OR IRRITATE YOUR FACE AS DO MISFIT BLADES. ALWAYS ASK FOR THIN GILLETTES

THIN GILLETTE BLADES 4 for 10¢

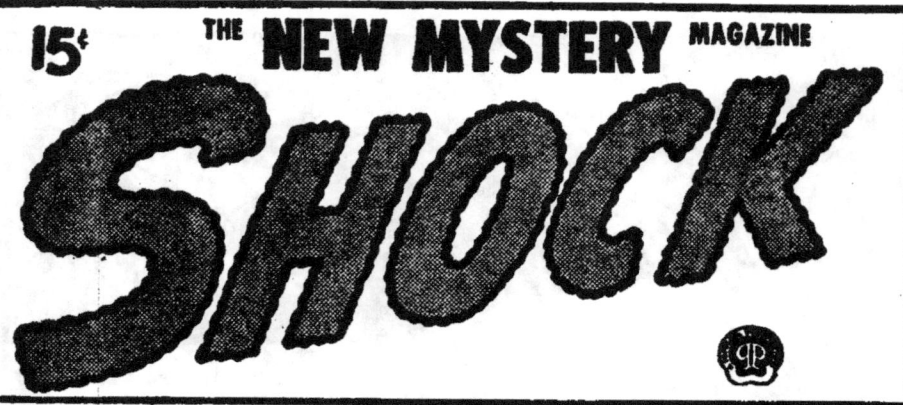

15¢

THE **NEW MYSTERY** MAGAZINE

SHOCK

Volume 1   May, 1948   Number 2

The next issue will be out June 2nd.

Published bi-monthly by New Publications, Inc., at 2256 Grove Street, Chicago 16, Illinois. Editorial and Executive Offices, 210 East 43rd Street, New York 17, N. Y. Henry Steeger, President and Secretary. Harold S. Goldsmith, Vice President and Treasurer. Application for second class entry, under the Act of March 3, 1879, pending at the Post Office at Chicago, Illinois. Copyright, 1948, by New Publications, Inc. This issue is published simultaneously in the Dominion of Canada. Copyright under International Copyright Convention and Pan-American Copyright Conventions. All rights reserved, including the right of reproduction, in whole or in part, in any form. Single copy, 15c. Annual subscription price for U.S.A., its possessions and Canada, 90c; other countries 25c additional. All correspondence relating to this publication should be addressed to 2256 Grove Street, Chicago 16, Illinois, or 210 East 43rd Street, New York 17, N. Y. When submitting manuscripts, enclose stamped self-addressed envelope for their return if found unavailable. Care will be exercised in the handling of unsolicited manuscripts, but no responsibility for their return is assumed. Any resemblance between any character appearing in fictional matter, and any person living or dead, is entirely coincidental and unintentional. Printed in U.S.A.

SLIM...STOUT...SHORT or TALL...

Lee Overalls   Lee Matched Shirts & Pants

Lee FITS 'EM ALL

Lee Union-Alls   Lee Shirts

One of the Many Reasons
Lee TOPS 'EM ALL

Regardless of your build, Lee "Tailored Sizes" give you perfect fit, lasting comfort and better appearance. Many other Lee Features result in satisfying Lee Work Clothes ownership for you.

BUY LEE WORK CLOTHES...AT LEADING STORES COAST TO COAST

THE H. D. LEE COMPANY, Inc.

Kansas City, Mo. • Minneapolis, Minn. • Trenton, N. J. • San Francisco, Calif.
South Bend, Ind. • Salina, Kansas

WORLD'S LARGEST MANUFACTURER OF UNION-MADE WORK CLOTHES

Blowing Off the Lid!

IN PART, the dictionary defines the the word "shock" as: "—a violent collision or impact; blow. A sudden and violent sensation, a sudden agitation of the mind; startling emotion. . ."

That sums up, succinctly, the policy of SHOCK Magazine. Unlike the average detective or mystery magazine, we are not content to merely take you away from humdrum everyday life for a few moments with the formula tale of crime and detection which you know so well. We aim to jolt you, to curl your toes and jar you with an emotional experience that you will never forget.

We do not believe that in the history of crime fiction has there been anything as new and really, truly, daringly different. There are many detective or mystery magazines but each is more or less a carbon copy of the other. With this publication, we offer you something completely unusual in the way of crime fiction.

Most readers have been through the mill with the "whodunits." They are an old story. Jaded appetites, hungry for something out of the ordinary in murder stories, will find it in the powerful tales we offer here.

Every story in SHOCK is written especially for us by a leading author in the crime-mystery field. It is not "just another crime story." It is an adventure in violence, in which you, the reader, move with the characters along the dark and twisting back alleys of crime in every nation in the world, and in every period of history. The only rule we have laid down for our writers is that they turn out the most powerful mystery-adventure stories they can—charged with high-voltage human interest.

The best tales of crime and violence have never been published, for fear of wounding sensitive minds. We feel that in this day and age of enlightenment, a realistic approach to the fascinating subject of crimes of pathological violence is no longer taboo. We are blowing off the lid. We are permitting our writers to pull out all stops and present their stories of men and women caught in the entangling web of crime and all its ramifications as it really happens, not as a superficially intellectual game of wits or a puzzle or amusing interlude in the lives of gay fiction folk who go around sticking their noses into crime business.

Sudden death by violence is not funny. It is not cute. It is shocking. It will not be treated lightly in these pages. You will find no all-too-familiar wise-cracking "private eyes" and their secretaries muddling through situations involving stock criminal characters who have been done to death, literally.

It is our intention to give you stories that are ordinarily considered too strong fare for the average reader. You will find no puppet characters, no hackneyed situations. The accent is on the bizzare and shocking in crime adventures happening to believable, recognizable people.

We hope that in reading these stories you will have—*the crime of your life!*

The Editor.

WHERE A MAN IS STILL IMPORTANT!

MACHINES are important. Inventions are important. But it's *men* who win wars and guard the peace.

No one knows that any better than the U.S. Army. That's why you'll find real men in the U.S. Infantry, Artillery, and Armored Cavalry.

These arms — the Combat Forces — are the fighting heart of the Army. Other branches exist only to support them. The Combat Soldier today has the finest equipment and transport ever devised — but he is also top-notch *as a man*. Courageous. Strong and hard physically. Alert. Intelligent.

If you're that kind of man, you'll find a welcome — and real comradeship — in the Combat Forces. It's a good life today, with high pay and training in many valuable skills and trades. If you're between 18 and 34 (17 with parents' consent) and above average physically and mentally, ask about the Combat Forces.

U. S. Army and U. S. Air Force Recruiting Service

Satan's Angel

It was here that I would
find my prey. . . .

*A smiling emissary of death, I sat among the
broken men of Skid Row—heartlessly playing eeny
meeny miney moe to choose which one would die!*

Startling Novel of a

Blood-Curdling Mission

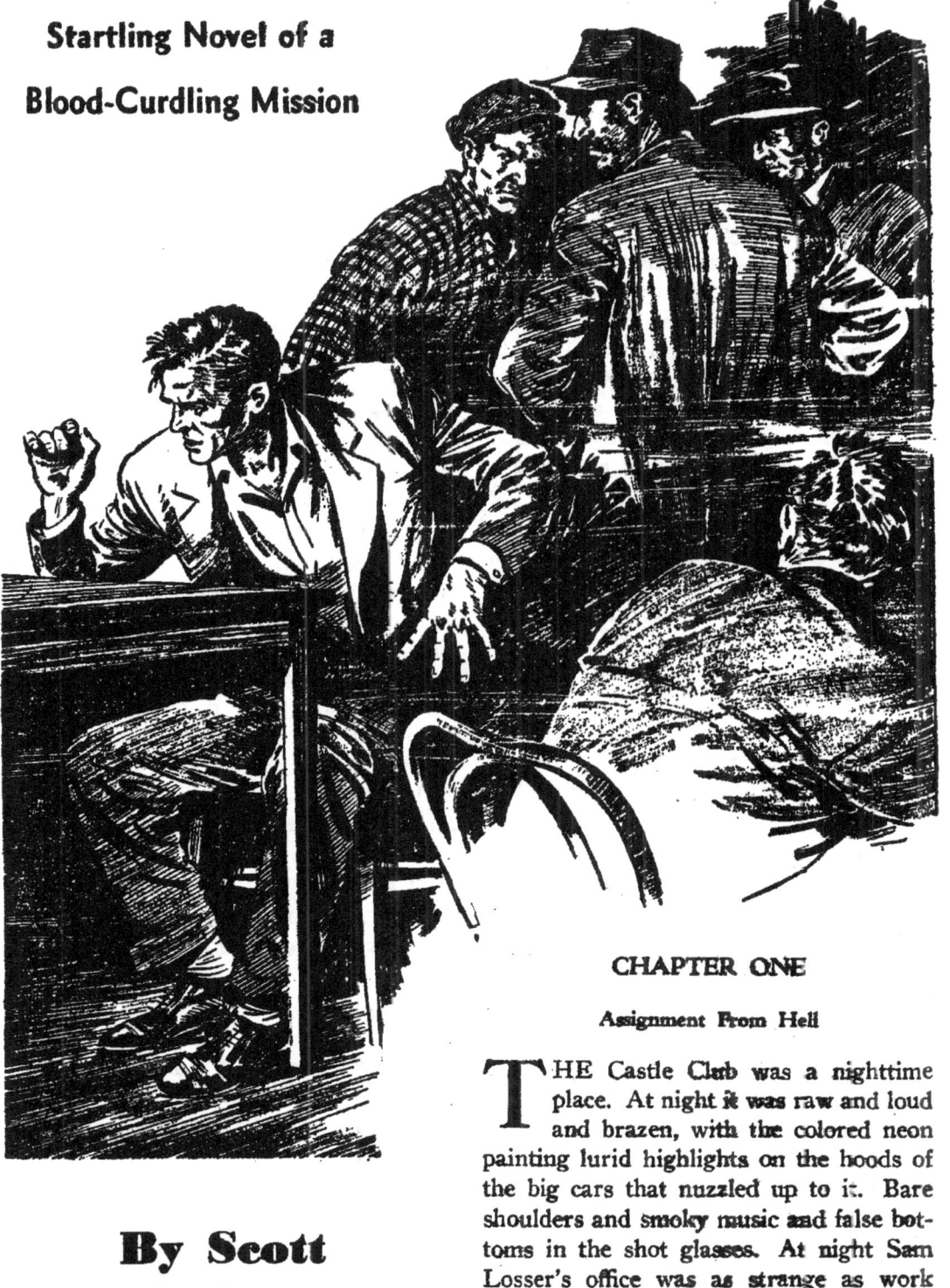

By Scott O'Hara

CHAPTER ONE

Assignment From Hell

THE Castle Club was a nighttime place. At night it was raw and loud and brazen, with the colored neon painting lurid highlights on the hoods of the big cars that nuzzled up to it. Bare shoulders and smoky music and false bottoms in the shot glasses. At night Sam Losser's office was as strange as work gloves on a chorine. It could have been the office of a hick lawyer. Golden oak and worn green carpet and a spittoon.

But in the daytime when the Castle Club was gray and dingy, when the tables were stacked, when a man in a dirty shirt checked the bottles on the backbar, and a slow old man knelt in the dirty gray rain and picked slivers of glass out of the parking lot—in the daytime Sam Losser's office became the only touch of reality.

He had a rolltop desk and an oak table at right angles to it. I sat on the other side of the oak table, my purse and gloves at my elbow. Sam's chair creaked. He held a slender cigar in his fat, muddy fingers, and huffed out a blue-gray column of smoke. He wore a baggy gray suit that matched his office. His bald head had a high sheen in the gray light from the big window.

With a slow movement, he reached out, spun the cigar in the ash tray, leaving a small neat cone of ash over the red glow.

His eyes were milky gray, almost opaque. He smiled and said, "Now you make like a soap opera, Ellen. Big tears yet."

"That doesn't answer the question," I said flatly, pleased that I could keep the quaver out of my voice.

"The question? Oh, you wanted to know where Johnny is, didn't you? If you did know, it wouldn't do you any good. Your brother has got to stay put for a while, Ellen. Johnny James is a name the cops would like to know."

"Aren't you supposed to have the cops in your pocket?"

He sighed. "Machines I can fix. A few gas stations knocked off I can fix. Lots of little things I can fix. Murder, no. Cops, they get eager about murder. So do all the kids in the D. A.'s office. I go to my people and say that to me it would be a personal favor if they let it slide. They say that I stay out of this one."

"Johnny didn't kill anybody," I said with a note of hysteria.

"Ellen, you are a good girl. You do nice clean secretarial work. Maybe you look at that white paper and black writing too long. Life is not black and white. life is full of shades of gray.

"What difference whether Johnny did it or not? Johnny is a very excitable boy. Johnny, he like a lot of dough in his pants. He likes nice things. You know how it is. Maybe he did and maybe he didn't kill anybody this time. Maybe next time he does. He's nervous."

I thought of my brother. Johnny with his clear reckless eyes and twisted smile and the ready fists. Johnny, who had worked in some mysterious capacity for Sam Losser ever since the dishonorable discharge he got for beating up his company commander.

On April fourteenth, three nights before, at two in the morning, three men had broken into the Connor Brothers Coal Company, smashed the safe and made off with a little over twenty thousand dollars. The watchman had died the following noon in the hospital from a depressed skull fracture. I had thought nothing of it until I found that Johnny had disappeared. He hadn't come back to his apartment. It was in the same building as mine. So I went to see Sam Losser.

"Did . . . those men rob the coal company because you told them to, Mr. Losser?"

He flattened his thick lips against his teeth as he smiled. His eyes were cold. "You got me wrong, Ellen. I got a tough business to run out here. I got to hire rough boys to help me. Sometimes, on their time off, those rough boys do a few things for excitement. Can I help that?"

"You won't help Johnny?"

He inspected the end of his cigar and rolled the ash off again. "You make it difficult, Ellen. Maybe I can help him. I don't know. If the pressure goes off the case, maybe I can help him a lot. If it stays on. . . ." He shrugged.

"Maybe the two men who were with Johnny are worth less to you than he is. Maybe if one of them. . . ."

He grinned, almost with delight. "Miss James, you got the same idea I got, but you got it in reverse. The two boys with Johnny are good boys. Steady boys. They been in the business years. Johnny, he's still a punk. Like I told you, he's exciteable. If the heat stays on I got to protect my investment by having them find Johnny. Just to make sure Johnny won't talk, he might be dead when they find him."

THE room spun and I felt my shoulders sag. Through thick mist Sam Losser's muddy face loomed and his faraway voice said, "You don't feel so good?"

I clung to consciousness, fought away the mists. I lifted my chin and said, "I feel fine."

He said softly, "You see, nobody was to get killed. Then it's okay. But the deal went wrong. So what was a good job is now a bad job. I give it to you straight, Ellen. If they smell around too close to me, I got to throw Johnny to them. In Johnny's pocket will be a lot of the dough and a sap that will fit the smashed place on the head of that watchman. Then the pressure is off."

"Did Johnny kill him?"

"I told you before, that doesn't make any difference."

He leaned back in his chair. It creaked again. I saw the thin gray threads of smoke rising toward the ceiling. If I could get Johnny, we could go away together. This thing would have driven the madness out of him. A new start. Johnny would become the same fine kid brother he had once been.

I said softly, "Isn't there anything I can do? Anything at all?"

He didn't answer. He stared at the rain pelting against his window. I said, "Suppose Johnny was a very good man,

very valuable to you, the same as the others. What would you do to take the heat off the three of them?"

He shrugged. "I might do a very dangerous thing. I might find some bum and have him killed and plant the stuff on him."

"Why don't you do that this time?"

"Johnny isn't worth the danger, Ellen. You figure you got a bum and all of sudden he's got friends who were with him the night he was supposed to be knocking off the watchman. Maybe somebody sees you contacting the bum. You got two murders instead of one."

I remembered all the things about Johnny. He was a good kid. Somewhere along the line he had gotten twisted. He could be set right.

Sam squashed the butt of the cigar, handling it delicately with his thick fingers. He smiled up at me. "Of course, if you could find us a bum for the part. . . ."

"Me?" I gasped.

"Sure. You get hold of some stew bum off River Street and take him to some room you get under the wrong name and pump him and make sure there won't be a hitch. Then you let me know, and we arrange a pickup and wrap him up for the cops."

I remembered the clear look Johnny used to have in his eyes. I remembered him, proud in his first long trousers. I remembered how his thin shoulders shook as I held him tight after our parents were killed at the grade crossing. I said:

"Suppose I do that. Then what?"

"Then you don't have to worry about Johnny. He can come back to work."

"But suppose I want to take him away from here? Suppose I think I can straighten him out?"

The rain was still pelting the windows, but a shaft of sun shone between the clouds, a thin line of it making a bright spot on the green rug. Sam pointed to it.

"You can straighten Johnny out the same way I can pick up that sunbeam and tie knots in it."

"But you will let him go?"

Sam looked at me. He shrugged. "Phone me here when you got the bum lined up. Phone from a pay station."

I stood up. He walked me to the door. He laughed as he closed it. As I went along the narrow hall I could hear the distant sound of his laughter. I walked across the floor, out the side door and climbed into my coupe. The old man had finished picking up the shattered glass.

The rain had stopped and I clicked on the wipers long enough to dash the standing drops from the windshield. My foot was shaking so badly that I fed the gas raggedly, clashing the gears as I drove out of the lot. . . .

From my apartment I phoned the office and told Mr. Hodges that I had seen the doctor and that he had ordered me to stay in bed for two days. Mr. Hodges was very pleasant about it. After I hung up, I went into the kitchenette, mixed myself a stiff drink and downed it. The warmth spread through me, but it didn't touch the ice chips in my heart.

How do you dress to find a man to be killed? Where do you go? Sam had mentioned River Street. I glanced at my watch. Four in the afternoon. Time to get dressed for death, to find a room, to have just enough to drink so that I could be hard and cold.

I looked over my clothes and picked a skirt that had shrunk during drycleaning. It would fit too tightly. Mesh stockings. Heels that were too high for comfort. A blouse that was frilly and cheap.

I spent a long time over the makeup. In the back of the bureau drawer I found the lipstick that was too deep. With it, I enlarged my lips, smearing it on heavily. Blue eye shadow. Black smeared on my lashes so thick that it left little beads on the end of each eyelash. I put on dangling earrings.

In the back of my closet was a cheap fibre suitcase that I had bought in a Chicago drugstore when my luggage had been stolen. I filled it with underthings that I had meant to throw away, but had forgotten. Another cheap blouse. Junk jewelry.

AT FIVE I took the phone off the hook, locked the apartment and caught a taxi at the corner. The driver looked me over appreciatively and said, "Let's make it a nice long ride, honey."

"Corner of River and State," I ordered.

The evening traffic was heavy. The driver was so busy trying to turn his head so that he could see my legs that twice we nearly piled into the back end of the car ahead.

River Street parallels the dock area. It is a street of small dives, missions, eroded hotels. State is the one decent street that cuts across it. It was heavy dusk when the driver let me out in front of the drugstore on the corner. I tipped him a quarter and he wanted me to have a beer with him. I walked off through the evening crowd, heading down River Street. I had to find a hotel where they weren't too particular.

I found it in the third block. Hotel Barton. Lobby one flight up. Rooms from one dollar.

The dim stairway smelled of dust and disinfectant, disease and poverty, perfume and gin. The small lobby was brilliantly lighted. An old man with a stubbled face sat asleep in a worn leather chair, a frayed newspaper across his chest. A battered table held stacked religious tracts. The rug was worn down through the faded rose pile to the brown strings that held it together.

A very thin, very sallow young man leaned with sharp elbows on the old desk and watched me as I walked across from the head of the stairs. I lifted my chin, smiled at him and walked with an exaggerated sway.

He looked at me with unblinking dark eyes. His white shirt was damp under the armpits and his lean fingers were dirty across the knuckles.

"I want to rent a room," I told him.

"Room with a shower. Buck seventy-five. In advance."

I paid him. He opened a book in front of me, handed me a pencil and pointed to a vacant line with a dirty thumb. *Lorene Vernon,* I wrote.

He slapped a key on the counter. "One eleven, Lorene. Right through that arch over there and down the hall. Next to the last one on your right. Pay every day in advance."

The key was fastened to a piece of greasy wood almost a foot long. I picked up the suitcase, walked down the hall.

I unlocked my door. The room was about ten by ten. One smeared window looked out across an airwell. There was a cheap maple bureau, chair, bed and bench. The lace curtains were torn and yellow with age. There was a strip of pale blue linoleum instead of a rug. The plaster walls were off-white.

One door opened into a shallow closet. The other opened into a tiny bathroom with stained plumbing, chipped fake tile and a naked overhead bulb. The only light in the bedroom was a bedside lamp in maple with a cardboard parchment shade with a silhouette of a ship in full sail. I sat on the bed and stared with unseeing eyes at the dusty floor beyond the strip of blue linoleum.

I sat in the room until after seven and then went out and ate in a small restaurant. I ate at the counter and realized that I was stalling over the food, dreading the actual moment when I'd have to begin my hunt for the nameless man who would, in the newspapers, become the man who had killed the old watchman at the coal company.

I was the pointing finger of death. The man I found would die. Outside the restaurant the coarse night life of the forty blocks along the river was beginning to roar. The juke boxes blared in the little joints.

After I paid the check, I walked out onto the sidewalk and headed down River Street. The three blocks near State were dotted with places that were large and noisy. I knew that I'd find my quarry in a quieter spot. Further along River the bright lights dimmed, the neon fizzed and crackled, the sidewalks were littered with filth.

Gradually I slowed my steps. Someplace here he would be, the lonesome man I would select for death.

There wasn't much traffic on River Street. A junk wagon went slowly by, a man hunched on the high seat, the hooves of the swaybacked horse making a clop, clop sound. Across the street from me a harsh bulb illuminated a black and white sign which said, *Jesus Saves!*

I glanced into the smeared window of a small bar. Four men stood at the bar. They were fairly well dressed. The bartender wore a clean white jacket. I had to walk further down River.

I heard a woman scream and I looked up at the black dead windows over the darkened store fronts. A woman was screaming in the dark. So what? All over the world women screamed.

My heels made a slow rhythmic beat against the dark pavement. I couldn't spend time worrying about a scream. I was worrying about death. I was an angel of death, and I walked the night streets of a great city looking for a man I would turn chill with my touch; looking for man-eyes that, because of me, would gaze sightless at the stars.

CHAPTER TWO

Eeny Meeny Miney Moe

THE soaped sign on a cracked window said, *Bar whiskey—1½ ounce shot—14c.* I went up the two stone steps, pushed the door open and walked into the place. It wasn't a place where women go. I felt that at once. There was no music, no heat, little light.

Two dark men stood at the bar. One turned and stared at me with a soundless whistle. The bartender, a vast broken man with dirty white hair paused for a moment, then continued wiping a glass on a torn towel.

Beyond the bar were circular tables and broken chairs. The room was filled with a vast silence. The silence of a tomb in which the not-yet-dead were buried, where they waited patiently for the death that would come.

One of the tables was empty. I sat down and the men at the other tables looked vaguely at me and looked away.

The room stank of unwashed bodies. It was here that I would find my prey.

The bartender came from behind the bar, looked down at me over the bulk of his huge belly. "We don't want no trouble."

"Bring me a bottle of beer. I don't want trouble. I just want beer."

He sighed, turned away and came back with an opened bottle and a water-spotted glass. He set them on the table, showed no glimmer of interest as I gave him a quarter and said, "Thank you very much."

The men sat motionless in the gloom. Hunched shoulders. Torn coats. Dirty bearded faces. Faces harrowed and lined and stained with what liquor had done to them. I knew that this was the last place they could sit inside, out of the cold spring wind; that when they no longer found the few cents to enable them to stay in this place, they would soon die. Some were old. And some were surprisingly young.

The angel of death sat among them. I wanted to giggle with hysteria. How shall I do it? Eeny meeny miney moe? Out goes Y - O - U! Let me do you a favor, boys. Who wants to die in a big way? Who wants to die with headlines? One at a time. Step up. Present your qualifications to the angel sans mercy.

The silent hunched shoulders. One of them made a hoarse sound in his throat and held his empty glass high. The bartender came over, stood silently until the man had counted out fourteen cents. Then he filled the glass from an unlabeled bottle.

The man looked down at the brim-full glass for long seconds. He snatched it suddenly, spilling a few drops, and set the empty glass down on the table again with a long, shuddering sigh. He bent over, fastened gray lips around the few spilled drops on the black wooden table and sucked them up noisily. He wiped his hand across his mouth and sat very still, his eyes closed.

As my eyes became accustomed to the light, I saw a younger man who was also alone at a table. He leaned back, his head against the wall, his mouth half open. He would have seemed asleep, but his eyes were half open and I had the feeling he watched me. I finished the beer, called the bartender over and said, "I want another beer. Serve it at that table over there."

"He hasn't got a dime in his pants, lady."

"Serve it over there, please."

He shrugged. When he moved away, I walked over to the other table. The young man's face seemed curiously blurred, the features indistinct. The stubble on his face was pale and colorless. His eyes were pale blue.

The bartender brought my beer. I told him to bring whatever the man usually drank. He brought back a shot glass filled to the brim. His hand was oddly steady for so old and shattered a man. I paid him.

I reached out and took hold of the arm of the young man and shook him. His head lolled and he looked at me stupidly. He said dimly, "Gloria. Hello, Gloria."

"I bought you a drink," I said, enunciating every word.

He peered at me, then looked slowly down toward the table top. His eyes narrowed as he saw the drink. A thin gray hand crept up across the table, moved gingerly toward the glass like some large timid insect.

His fingers touched the smooth glass, stopped. Slowly he bent over until his mouth was inches from the rim. With both hands he lifted the precious glass, touched it to his lips and drank. When it was empty the glass clattered back onto the table top.

"Thanks, Gloria," he mumbled. The voice came from a long way off. A distant voice. A dead voice.

"Can you walk?" I said, shaking him again.

He didn't answer. Long seconds passed. "Where we going?" he asked weakly.

"Will you come with me?" I asked.

He looked at me then, his forehead wrinkled with the effort of trying to think clearly. "Taking me home, Gloria. Long time ago. Used to take me home. Before you died. . . ."

"Stand up," I said, standing myself and tugging at his arm.

He clawed at the wall, pushed at the table and managed to stand erect. He weaved heavily against me and I staggered under his weight. Together we went toward the front door. I risked a glance at the bartender. He was wiping a glass.

I bumped the door open with my shoulder. It had started to rain again.

He teetered on the top step, slipped out of my hands as I tried to grab him. He smashed against the wet sidewalk and was still. When I lifted his head I saw the blood was running from his mouth. Surprisingly, he seemed stronger. With one hand on my shoulder, he pulled himself up, lurched over against a wall, hitting it with force that drove the wind out of him. He gasped for a moment and then said, "Where we go, Gloria?"

"This way."

Five long blocks to the Barton. Once he started coughing. I had to support him until the paroxysm was over. It sapped his strength and he leaned more heavily against me. The rain soaked into his clothes, releasing an ancient smell of cheap, wet cotton, soiled wool.

I GUIDED him inside the lower hallway of the Barton and gave him a few minutes to catch his breath. The stairs were narrow and steep. Once, near the top, he swayed dangerously back, and it took every ounce of my strength to swing him forward again. He blundered up the last few steps and fell on his hands and knees. He stayed in that position until he felt me grasp his arm. I got him back on his feet.

The white young man behind the desk slapped my key down and looked with disgust at the man who stood behind me, swaying, his eyes almost shut.

I took the key, steered the man down the hallway, unlocked the door and pushed him in. He blundered over toward the bed, sat heavily on it as I slammed the door and locked it on the inside.

He sat on the edge of the bed, his elbows on his knees, staring down at the floor. His matted hair was wet with the rain. The water dripped from him.

Death would be a boon to this one. Death was coming to him very soon even if I hadn't selected him.

The instructions from Sam were to find out what this clod had been doing at the time the murder was committed. In order to tell me anything, he'd have to be sobered up. He coughed again, and the deep, rasping convulsion shook him.

Suddenly I hated him. I walked over to him and hit him on the side of the face with all my strength. The blow knocked him back on the bed. He looked up at me and his eyes rolled. He squinted with the effort of trying to see me.

"Not Gloria," he mumbled. "You're not Gloria."

There was dull heartbreak in his voice. I knelt and unlaced his shoes. Once they had been shoes. They were shapeless and dirty gray. They had the plupy feel of old newspaper. There was no lace in one of them. I pulled them off. He wore no socks. His ankles and feet were painfully thin, gray-white and dirty.

He half helped me as I pulled him up to a sitting position, wrestled his arms out of the torn tweed jacket, stained with age. Under the jacket he wore a cheap red sweater, no shirt.

I yanked the sweater up over his head. Every rib was visible. His skin was a muddy gray. He looked as forlorn as a plucked chicken. He shivered. I couldn't think of him as a man. He was something that was hurt and dying.

His belt was too big for him and the buckle was broken. It was knotted tightly. I helped him with the knot, grasped his trouser legs and pulled them off. His shorts were gray and worn. His legs were like gray stalks. The muscles he had once had were like limp gray string. His eyes were vacant, his mouth half open.

I pulled hard on his wrist and he stood up, wavering. I tugged him into the tiny bathroom, turned on the shower and pushed him under it. He shivered as the water hit him. I left him standing numbly under the shower and I went in, kicked his clothes into a corner and sat on the bed.

He fell heavily. When I ran in he was half in and half out of the shower. There was no waking him. I patted him dry with a towel and dragged him back into the bedroom.

After three tries I managed to get him up onto the bed. He was like lead. I guessed that once he had been a big man— before liquor had melted the flesh off of him. I covered him over. His breathing was heavy. His pulse was less than sixty. His hands were like ice.

His papers were in a cheap wallet in the left hip pocket of his trousers. Not many papers. Just the life record of a man about to die. A driver's license that had expired. Eric Norstram. Born July 10, 1917. Six feet. 185 pounds. Address— 1820 Bellaire. Not a bad address. Not a good one. But not bad.

Social Security card. Taken out in 1937. Twenty when he had taken it out. A few soiled business cards. *Imperial Valve Corporation, Detroit. Eric Norstram, Sales Representative.* A cracked photograph. A small woman with a lean, vital face.

The cards were damp from the rain that had soaked us. I spread them out to dry on the bureau.

There was an extra blanket in the bottom drawer of the bureau. I made myself a hard bed on the floor and, after turning out the light, lay down fully dressed, my coat over me. Norstram's heavy breathing filled the room. I remember thinking that it would be impossible for me to ever get to sleep, and the next moment the gray dawn outlined the window.

I couldn't go back to sleep. I was stiff and sore. Norstram hadn't moved. I felt his forehead. It was like flame. His lips were cracked and dry. His lungs rattled as he breathed.

After I came back from breakfast he had half regained consciousness, but he had no idea where he was. Fever had taken the place of alcohol. He mumbled endlessly about Gloria. I pulled the chair over to the bed and listened to him.

It wasn't hard to piece the situation together. Gloria had been his wife. He drank too much. She threatened to leave him. He still didn't straighten out. She left him.

He stopped drinking, drove over to Cleveland and got her. On the way back the car skidded into a telephone pole. Gloria was killed. He wasn't even scratched. That was over a year ago. Two weeks later he had lost his job. He hadn't been entirely sober since that moment.

A dozen times he relived the accident in the midst of delirium. Once he thought I was Gloria and in his efforts to protect me from the crash, he made a wild swing and his bony wrist hit me under the ear, sweeping me off the chair. He yelled hoarsely and his eyes were wild. A girl in the next room hammered on the wall, yelling that she couldn't sleep. I paid no attention to her.

At eleven I went back to my apartment, got more cash and a large box of sulpha left over from the time I had an ear infection. I propped him up and gave him the prescribed dosage. He gulped the water hungrily.

In the afternoon he slept. I went down the street to a drugstore and phoned Sam.

"Sam? This is the girl who talked to you yesterday."

"Oh! What's the report?"

"I've got what you—suggested. But I can't deliver until maybe the day after tomorrow. I'll let you know. Will it be okay?"

"It'll be fine. When you're ready, just let me know. The best deal will be about two in the morning. Take the item to a corner I'll tell you when you phone again. We'll arrange pickup. The item you got is—clean?"

"Absolutely. Nobody will ever miss it."

"You're a smart girl."

"Thanks, Sam." I hung up and went back to the room.

CHAPTER THREE

Dress Up for Death

ERIC NORSTRAM still snored. His forehead didn't seem so hot. At dusk I went out and brought him back a bowl of soup. I turned on the lamp, set the soup on the table and shook him gently. "Eric! Eric!" I said.

"Uh? Wha you want?"

"Wake up, Eric."

The light shone across his gray face. He opened blue startled eyes and looked up at me. A puzzled look crossed his face. "Who are you?" he asked weakly.

"Never mind that. Here. Sit up and drink this. If you're too weak I'll feed it to you."

He squirmed into a half-sitting position. He still looked puzzled, but he reached for the spoon. I held the bowl while he spooned the soup into his mouth with a shaking hand. When it was gone he sank back with a grateful sigh.

"Cigarette?" he said weakly.

I lit one for him, handed it to him. He sucked hungrily at it. "Tastes funny," he said.

"It should. You've been sick. Had a fever. You're full of sulpha."

"I feel hot."

"The fever isn't as bad as it was."

The blue eyes fastened on me again. "Say, who are you?"

"Just a girl who took care of you while you were the sickest."

He looked around the room. "This your place?"

"It's a room in the Barton on River Street."

He looked at me with a funny expression. "Oh!"

"Maybe you've been sick for days without knowing it. Maybe you were sick as long ago as, say the fourteenth."

"Fourteenth? Of what month?"

"This month."

"Look, I got a vague idea this is 1948. Don't pin me down to months."

"Where do you live?"

He rubbed a shaking hand across the colorless stubble on his cheek. "Got me there, too. For a while I had a bed for two bits a night on Willis Street, but that seems like a long time ago. A guy let me sleep sometimes in the watchman's cabin on a freight dock, but I don't know whether that was before or after the flophouse. Where did you find me, sister?"

"On your face on the sidewalk."

"That's called the Norstram position, sister."

"The name is Lorene Vernon."

"Okay, Lorene. What's the angle?"

"Does there have to be an angle?"

"Isn't there always? I'm a bum, Lorene. I don't kid myself about that. I haven't got a dime. So why spend your time taking care of me?"

"Maybe I'd take care of any sick thing. A sick cat even."

He looked at me for long seconds. "Hey, maybe you would. Maybe you would."

"Gloria would have, wouldn't she?"

He jumped as though I had stuck a pin in him. "What do you know about Gloria?" he asked hoarsely.

"Oh, you talked about her a lot. You've got the idea you killed her or something."

"I did."

I curled my lip as I looked at him. "If you want to be a lush, I suppose self pity is as good an excuse as any."

I thought for a moment he was going to get angry. He sank back on the pillow. "I don't fight with anybody," he said softly. "Is there a drink in the house?"

"No."

"Will you go get a bottle?"

"No."

"Then I'll go get one."

"In the first place you're pretty weak. In the second place I took your clothes out and stuffed them into a trash barrel."

For the first time he smiled. "How nice of you!"

"Tomorrow I'll buy you some more."

"Thank you, Lady Bountiful."

"Shut up!"

Lady Bountiful! Bountiful with death, my lad. Ashamed to send you off to be killed in your sad rags. She salves her conscience by buying you a new cheap suit and a new cheap shirt. Maybe she'll spend a few minutes picking out a blue figured tie. Blue to match your eyes. A tie to die in, chump. A pretty tie to match your dead blue eyes.

I walked over to the window, stared across at the brick wall which grew more dim as the dusk became heavier. When I turned, he was on his back, staring up at the ceiling. When I spoke he wouldn't answer. His mouth had an odd set look.

I paused at the door and said, "I'm going out to eat. The cigarettes are on the bureau. The shower I shoved you into last night only washed some of the dirt off. A scrubbing wouldn't hurt you. I'm locking the door on the outside. I don't know when I'll be back." I yanked the door shut, locked it, and stuffed the key with board attached into my big purse.

After I ate, I went back to my own apartment, put the phone back on the cradle, took a long hot bath, scrubbed the makeup off and drifted off into dreamless sleep.

IN THE morning, disguised again, I took a bus downtown, ordered a breakfast to go, and took it to Eric at the Barton. He was still sullen, but the shakes weren't as bad. There was even a bit of color in his sallow cheeks under the beard.

"I'll get you some clothes. Better give

me the sizes—so they'll fit," I added.

Making allowances for the weight he had lost, he gave the sizes and I wrote them down on the back of an envelope.

Just as I left, he said, "Why are you doing this, Lorene?" He was propped up on one elbow, his expression earnest, his eyes on mine.

"How should I know? You were sick. Now you're better. I'll buy you some clothes. Maybe you'll take me out to-night. Big date."

I caught the puzzled look in his eyes as I pulled the door shut.

Twenty-two fifty for a gray suit. I gave them the inseam measurement and waited while they fixed the trousers. Thirty cents for socks. Five-fifty for shoes. One eighty-five for a white shirt. Sixty-five cents for a blue figured tie. A dollar for shorts, a dollar six for razor, blades and shaving cream. Ten cents for a comb.

Dress up for death, Eric. You want to look good on that slab. Maybe I was silly. I bought him a wallet for two dollars, spent another dime for a nail file and forty-five cents for a decent handkerchief.

Loaded down with bundles, I got back to the Barton at noon. He had moved from the bed over to the one chair. He sat with the cotton blanket wrapped around him, smoking and staring out the window. He turned quickly as I unlocked the door. I dumped the pile of bundles on the bed. I managed to give him a cheery smile. "Your wardrobe, sire."

I saw a dull red flush under the color-less beard. "It's money tossed into a hole in the ground, Lorene."

"I can stand it."

"I'm shot, Lorene. Inside and out. I've been sitting here thinking."

"That's the way people get into trou-ble. Thinking." He could think and I couldn't. If I stopped to think, I would see him dead. He would be dead soon.

"Pretty yourself up, Eric. I'll be back

to see you again in about an hour."

I went to the drugstore and phoned Sam. "This is that girl again. Delivery okay tonight?"

A few seconds silence. "Yeah. Can do. Southwest corner of River and Gardener at two in the morning. It'll help if the package is loaded. You know what I mean."

"Yes I do. And what about—our friend?"

"He'll be back in town by ten tomorrow morning."

I hung up. I had no appetite for lunch. I walked through the gray warm day and everyone in the city, everyone in the world, was a stranger to me. I wondered how executioners feel the day before they must release the trap, pull the switch, swing the gleaming axe. Do they fasten a loose smirk on their lips and say to themselves, 'We all got to die sometime?'

I walked with blind eyes and a heart that beat slowly. When I passed the places that made the air rank with the smell of greasy food, I tasted quick nausea in my throat. The timid angel. The faltering hand of death. Hold still, sir. This hurts me more than it does you. Hold still for death. Assume the angle.

But it was for Johnny. Bold Johnny with a laugh like a shining note of silver, eyes that are mad and wonderful. The kid brother. Take care of him, Ellen James. Take care of your brother. You are your brother's keeper.

Eric Norstram turned from the bureau mirror as I walked into the room. His face was flushed with shame and pleasure. He stood awkwardly in his new clothes, with the weakness of one who has been ill. He looked as though he had recently been discharged from a hospital. His clean-shaven cheeks and jaw were sallow-white, his hair combed neatly. The suit hung on him in folds, but fit perfectly across the shoulders.

"You look wonderful, Eric!" I said. Fit for death, my love. Dressed to meet the fates.

"I've been staring into this mirror for fifteen minutes," he admitted guiltily. "I've been wondering if it's me. Inside me a voice keeps telling me that if I keep the suit pressed, I can put the bite on a lot of old friends for a few bucks. I keep telling the voice to shut up."

"Are you being virtuous?" I asked scornfully. "Brother, in ten days those clothes will look like the ones I stuffed in the barrel."

He sat on the edge of the bed. "You're a pretty hard kid, aren't you, Lorene?"

"I don't kid myself."

"Once a bum always a bum. Is that it?"

"Something like that."

"I'm hungry. Can you stand the fee for a steak?"

"For as many as you can eat, Eric." Be nice to him, Ellen. The condemned man ate a hearty meal. Anyway, Eric, they won't come in and shave your leg and the back of your head to make a good contact for the electrodes. You won't know a thing about it.

He staggered from weakness as we turned into the small diner. For a moment he rested heavily against me, then took his hand away hurriedly and said, "I tripped."

We sat at the counter. While I had coffee he had two orders of steak and french fries, apple pie and ice cream. He ate with steady determination, the muscles at the corner of his jaw bunching with each measured bite.

Over his coffee he said, "I was a pretty solid guy when I blacked out, Lorene. This morning I was looking at my legs. They look like I was half sparrow. I got a lot of weight to get back."

I smiled. "Is that what you were doing? I thought you were laying a firm foundation for the next binge."

For a moment he looked as though I had slapped him. "I can't figure you, Lorene."

"What is there to figure? If you want your head patted and if you want somebody to tell you that you can stop drinking, go to a clinic. I'm no reformer. I'm just setting you up for the next bout."

He stared down into the dregs of his coffee. "You're a funny one," he said.

"I'm a scream," I said.

"What do you want to do now?" he asked.

"Well, since I've put you back together, bit by bit, you can return the favor by being an agreeable escort for the rest of the day."

He smiled ruefully. "I'll need a nap in the middle of the afternoon."

"Favor granted."

"You know, Lorene, you don't talk like—"

"Like a gal with a room at the Barton?"

"Something like that. I got the way I was when you—found me, because, well, life gave me a pretty rough deal. Something on the same line must have happened to you."

I looked away. "Mr. Norstram, our delicate friendship is based on not getting involved in serious conversation. It makes my head hurt."

I paid the check. He took my arm as we left. His hand was surprisingly strong and firm. Out on the sidewalk he yawned. "I've got to collapse for a time, Lorene."

We went to the desk and I handed him the key. We moved away from the desk and he said, "You trust me, don't you?"

"Why not? Go get your sleep."

"What will you do?"

"How does that concern you?"

I watched him go through the arch, headed back to my room. I knew he was angry with me because the back of his neck was red. I made a mental note to give him the money for a haircut. But what did it matter? Is there any rule of procedure for hair length on a corpse?

I went to a cheap double feature. I didn't know the names of the pictures when I walked in, and I still didn't know them when I came out three hours and twenty minutes later.

Instead of the screen, I saw a car with Eric struggling in the back seat. Two men held him. I stood and watched the car drive away. The scene shifted. A prowl car stood, engine running, by a deserted lot. The spotlight shone on a body. A cop kneeling by the body said loudly, "A roll of bills and a sap. He was shot in the head. Call Homicide."

I knocked on the door. The key grated in the lock and Eric opened it. His eyes were puffed with sleep. He looked cross and upset.

He reached out, caught my wrist and pulled me toward him. Through tight lips he said, "What the hell are you doing in a setup like this?"

I yanked my hand away. "Is that your business?"

"Can't I make it my business?"

"You're a lush. You can't stop thinking about liquor long enough to have any other business."

His shoulders sagged. "Okay, okay. I'm wearing the clothes you bought. You're the boss."

"Let's go. I need a drink."

He pulled on his suit coat and I locked the door behind us.

CHAPTER FOUR

Delivered—One Corpse

WE WALKED over to State and went into a cocktail lounge, sat at a small circular red leather booth in a corner. Mirrors on the walls disguised the essential cheapness of the place. I glanced at Eric. He was very pale. He held onto the edge of the table so tightly that his knuckles were as white as the napkins.

"Martini for me," I said. "What do you want, Eric?"

"Ginger ale," he said in a hoarse voice.

The waiter went away. "Virtuous, aren't you?" I said.

"A drink would—upset me," he said carefully.

I laughed. "That's a good word for it."

When the drinks came, I took a sip of mine, shoved it over toward him. "Eric, I think they use cheap gin in their Martinis. Take a sip and see what you think."

His hand flashed out and he grasped the stem of the glass. He half lifted it and then set it down again. I could see that every nerve end in him was screaming for the warm embrace of alcohol. Slowly he loosened his fingers. "I couldn't tell."

Slowly I drank the rest of it. His eyes stayed on the glass until the last drop of amber fluid was gone. He swallowed thickly.

"Damn you," he whispered. "Damn you! You know what you're doing!"

"Doing? Me?" I asked with mock surprise. "What on earth would I be doing?"

"Let's get out of here," he said hoarsely.

I gave him a ten. He paid the check and, when he tried to give me the change, I told him to hold onto it.

I made him take me to two more cocktail places. Each time, as I drank, perspiration put a sheen on his high, pale forehead, on his upper lip. His pale blue eyes were haunted. I began to worry for fear that by the time two o'clock came around, he would still be stone sober. Sam wouldn't care for that.

I was too nervous to eat very much. He had a heavy meal, seeming to gain strength from it.

"Now what?" he asked when we had finished. I glanced at my watch. Eight thirty. Five and a half hours to go.

"Your choice," I said, trying to smile. "We'll walk."

Down River to State. Down State to the docks. Over the waterfront alley between the docks and the warehouses. One long pier was empty.

"Let's go out there," he said.

Our heels made hollow sounds on the big planks of the dock after we got beyond the concrete. The river ripples made lapping sounds against the piling. The wind off the river was cool and moist. Far out in the channel two barges towed by a tug were going up the river. Their running lights had red and green halos formed by the mist.

"You're quiet," I said. I spoke too loudly.

He started. "Guess I am. A lot to think about, Lorene. A hell of a lot. When you go a long time without thinking, there's a lot to catch up on."

It's not fair, I thought. It's not fair. You are not supposed to think. You have

been a symbol. You have been something I rescued from one death in order to give you to another.

I shivered. "Cold! Let's walk some more."

Something in the night had given him strength. He walked with his chin up, his hand firm on my arm. His strides were long and he seemed unconscious of my difficulty in keeping up with him.

When we passed a street light I looked at my watch. A few minutes after ten. I stopped. "What's the matter?" he asked.

"A girl can only walk so far. One more block and you'd be carrying me."

"I feel strong enough to do that, too."

"Me for a drink."

He hesitated. "A movie maybe?"

"A drink, pardner. Foot on the rail stuff."

We were three blocks from River. I led the way and he followed along meekly. The place looked all right. Pickled pine. Shining brass. I led the way back to a rustic booth in a darkened corner.

The waiter came over. "Ginger ale for me," Eric said. "How about you, Lorene?"

I knew what I had to do. "Straight rye. Water chaser." I had never tried to drink straight liquor in my life. I knew I was right by the look in Eric's eyes when I placed the order.

The waiter brought it, along with the check.

Eric looked at the shining shot glass as he sipped his ginger ale. I didn't look at him. Slowly I pushed the shot glass over to him. "You better take this too, Eric. It'll do you good."

My hands were resting on the edge of the table. His thin hands slipped across the table. He grabbed my wrists so tightly that he hurt me. He looked into my face. He was white and his eyes were like the blue flame that plays over hot coals.

He spoke through clenched teeth. "Funny aren't you? Funny like a new boil."

"You're hurting my wrists!"

He didn't hear me. "Why are you doing this to me? Why?"

I lifted my chin. "Because you can't take it."

His fingers relaxed on my wrists. He picked up the shot glass with a steady hand. He lifted it to his lips, sipped. His eyes had a strange look. He held the sip of rye in his mouth, deliberately took out the handkerchief I had bought him and spat the sip of rye into it.

He took my wrists again, and his touch was gentle. "Lorene, we despise what we are. Both of us. Please, Lorene, listen to me. We hate what we are. This is a way out for us. For the two of us. You just saw how strong I can be when I'm with you. You're the only chance I've got, Lorene. Please. I can get a job selling. You wouldn't know it right now, but I'm a good salesman. People like me. I can get a job. Let's get out of this crummy town together. The two of us."

His face had lost that blurred, indistinct look. The loose lines around his mouth had firmed.

"Darling, life has done something foul to both of us. I want to marry you."

How is it, Ellen, to sit across the table from death, and death has warm fingers on your wrists, death has a look of life in its eyes that will soon be shut forever? This thing you have created, this body that you have given life and hope.

I looked into his eyes and I was suddenly horribly tired. There was no thought behind my words. "You have no right to talk like this."

"I know I haven't," he said humbly.

"You don't even know what I mean! You don't even know what I mean!"

Suddenly my voice was shrill and the tears were running down my cheeks. The tangled, fumbling words came out. Slowly as he made sense out of them, the look

went out of his eyes; they went blank and dead. They became the eyes that I had seen when he picked himself up, bleeding, from the sidewalk.

He let go of my wrists and leaned back. "Lorene isn't your name, then?"

"My name is Ellen James. I work as a secretary." The tears were suddenly gone and all emotion was drained out of me. We were strangers again.

"And you were supposed to turn me over to these people so they won't make a fall guy out of your brother. They would have killed me instead of him?"

"Yes."

His smile wasn't a good thing to look at. "You were doing so beautifully up until now, Miss James. Why did you suddenly decide to tell the truth?"

"I don't know."

"When I made my silly offer a few minutes ago, I thought I was making it to Lorene Vernon who has a room in the Barton. Instead I was making it to the very proper Miss James. The homicidal Miss James."

"Don't," I said weakly.

"Relax, Miss James. We'll call it a temporary lack of balance on my part. Where was this two o'clock transfer supposed to take place?"

"Southwest corner of River and Gardener."

"What kind of a kid is this brother of yours?"

"He was a good kid, Eric. Really a good kid. Something just went wrong with him somehow. I don't know where or when. He's—twisted inside now. He frightens me."

He said gently, "You must love him a great deal to do—this sort of thing for him."

"Love him? I don't know. I love what he used to be. I hate what he is."

"Suppose somebody who knows my name saw us together?"

"I was going to take that chance. It would be okay, if it helped Johnny."

His lips curled. "You shouldn't have told me, you know."

"I had to."

"You didn't figure all the angles, Miss James. I'm no longer your pigeon, and while you're getting another fall guy, I'll be back up to here in rye."

"Then everything you said was an act too, Eric. All that guff about me being the only one to help you. I've straightened you out for a long time, haven't I? . . . Good-by, Eric. Happy dreams."

Before he could stop me, I picked up my purse and hurried out. It was raining again. The rain mingled with the tears that came. I knew no reason why there should be tears. I ran until my heart pounded and a great pain came in my side. Gasping, I went into a cigar store and shut myself in the phone booth.

"Sam? This is that girl again."

"What's wrong?"

"The delivery got fouled up, Sam."

Long seconds. Heavy sigh. "I can't stop the boys from showing. It's after eleven now. They'll be there on schedule. Unless you can find somebody else in the meantime, show up yourself and tell them it's off."

"Okay, Sam."

I hung up, bought cigarettes at the counter.

I tried, Johnny. I'll do it yet, Johnny. With somebody else. Somebody who is . . . further gone. Somebody without blue eyes and strong fingers and that look of hope and pleading. Maybe, in my shoes, Johnny, you couldn't have done it either. I hope not.

TWO O'CLOCK. Lagging feet took me to the corner. The wind had come up. Rain whipped around the brutal stone shoulders of the gray buildings. The windows were blank black sockets where eyes

had once been. The night life of River Street that had been a solid brassy blare at midnight was beginning to fade. The city gagged, coughed and seemed to change position in its sleep.

In an alley a girl cried, flatly, tonelessly. A bottle smashed against the bricks. A man stood with his cheek against the wet cold metal of the street sign.

I crossed over to the southwest corner. A man stood in the shadows. I stood and felt that he watched me. There was something familiar about his stance.

Three steps closer. "Eric! What do you want here?"

Tired voice. "That was the arrangement, wasn't it? Never let it be said that Norstram fouled up a lady in distress."

"But you can't!"

"Can't what? I'm not being a tragic figger, honey. This is just a nice clean way to do it. This way, maybe I accomplish something."

I grabbed his wet coat, pulled at him. "Get away from here, Eric! Get away! You've been drinking."

He laughed tonelessly. "That's where you're wrong, honey. Very wrong. I haven't had a drink."

A big car came down the street at a fast rate. The shocks smacked against the frame as it hit the potholes in the street. It slid smoothly up to the curb.

"Ah, my taxi," Eric said. "A short ride to the Styx."

He stepped toward the door that swung open. I grabbed his arm, pulled hard, held tightly in spite of his efforts to free himself.

A man got out of the car, came quickly across the sidewalk.

"What the hell goes on?"

"Johnny!" I gasped.

"Sam told me you got me a pigeon." Johnny stood in a half crouch. "Nice work, Sis. Come on, you."

"Don't take him, Johnny! Don't take

him!" I pleaded. "He's not the one."

"You're quite a joker, Sis," he said, showing white teeth. He yanked my hands off Eric's sleeve, shoved Eric roughly toward the car. He put a hand against my shoulder, pushed me away violently and said, "You're all through with this deal, Sis. Keep your nose out. Thanks for the pigeon. And I'm not coming back. I got a big arrangement on the Coast with Sammy."

Eric turned in time to see me nearly fall from Johnny's rough push. He said, "Hey, what do—"

Johnny cursed and hit him heavily in the mouth. The quick blood showed black in the faint light of the streetlamp. As Eric sagged, Johnny tumbled him into the back seat of the car. The door slammed, the motor raced and the sedan roared off.

I turned and ran. I sobbed aloud as I ran. The light of the drugstore was incredibly distant. As I ran it seemed to recede from me.

I managed to get a nickle out of my purse, dialed the operator.

She connected me quickly. "Police Headquarters, Sergeant Gray."

"Emergency. A black Pontiac sedan, license Y 8463, kidnapped a man named Eric Norstram three minutes ago on the corner of River and Gardener. They headed north on Gardener. They're going to kill Norstram."

With infuriating slowness, he made me repeat the license. He cut me off for a few moments, came back on the line. "Okay, we got it on the radio. If you're right on the time, they won't make it out of town. Now, who was in the car?"

"I recognized one man. John James. He works for Sam Losser who owns the Castle Club on Route 34. John James was one of the three who robbed Connor Coal."

Sergeant Gray whistled. "You sure?"

"Sam Losser told me."

"We better come and get you and bring

you in here. You may be a little unpopular. Who are you?"

"Ellen James. John is my brother."

"Where do we find you?"

Sam Losser

I gave him the address. I hung up slowly. My hands were cold with perspiration. During the few moments I had before the white sedan pulled up in front, I scrubbed off most of the heavy makeup.

I sat alone in the back seat. The thick shoulders of the two men in uniform were like a wall of blue stone.

A dim impression of a large room, white tile, golden oak, cigar smoke. Sergeant Gray had a kind, florid face.

"Better sit down, Miss James."

"Did. . . did. . . ?"

"Yes. Got them at the bridge near Anderson Avenue. There was stuff from the coal company safe in the car. They're coming in now. The others. Not your brother. He tried to run for it. . . ."

There was a sharp smell in my nose and I fought feebly to push away the hand that held the sharp smell so close to me. "Take it easy," a voice said gently.

I opened my eyes and looked into Gray's face. My voice sounded far away. "Where is . . . Eric?"

Gray grinned and winked at somebody beyond me. He said, "Lady, that ain't exactly a sofa cushion you got your head on."

THE END

The Wise Guy

By John Bender

Were those Jerries sore when we took those foxhole babes away from them!

I DON'T suppose I've ever been any sicker in my life. The sky went round and round, with bright lights and bells stabbing through the night, and everything seemed to be fighting its way up my throat.

How long it lasted, I don't know. Forever, it seemed; dragging the strength right up out of my shoes, while I tried to support myself against the tree. Then I just gave up and let go—of the tree, and myself and everything—and the lieutenant of detectives became just another blur in the darkness.

I didn't cry. But my eyes were leaking salt by the time I'd finished, weak and helpless, with my heart pounding its terrible rhythm against my ribs.

Madden, the police lieutenant, helped me to my feet and got me away from the curb. He was a tall man, big and heavy, a comfortable block to lean on there in the strange quiet of the ghastly night.

"You're Mort Reeves," he said, the

Locked deep in the dungeon of his soul was a secret that should never be freed.

way you'd read a time-table. "That right?"

I must have nodded. He started moving me on my dead legs, down the sidewalk, away from the mess I'd made. He kept both arms around me, nodding with his head in the direction of a parked police car.

We went past it, with him walking me a little faster. My head began to find my shoulders, and the blood started running again in my legs.

We came back to the police car and he helped me in, setting me on the cushioned seat so that my legs draped comfortably outside. He went around and got in on the driver's side, then reached over and brought my legs in, and closed the door.

A match flicked to life. "Cigarette?" he asked.

I told him no, forcing the word out.

He reached into the glove compartment. I heard the slosh of liquid, the tinkle of metal striking a metal container. "Maybe this'll get rid of that bad taste."

The sharp smell of the whiskey cut into the sensitive membranes of my nose. I half-coughed, half-sneezed, but I took the flask and let the fire of the liquor run down into my throat, cutting the constriction there.

"Better, eh?" He screwed the metal cap on and put the flask away, but he wasn't in any hurry. He finished almost all of his cigarette before he said, "Tough, fella." There wasn't any friendliness in his voice.

I could see him better now—a thick-faced, solid man in a dark gray overcoat. His eyes caught the glow of his cigarette and made tiny points of light in his face.

"Thanks," I said. "I'm—I'm okay now."

"Sure." He nodded. "Sure. Take your time with it. Whenever you're ready."

I cleared my throat. "What do you want to know?"

"What do you want to tell me?" He threw the cigarette away and got out a small notebook. "All of it. As much as you know."

Well, how much did I know, I asked myself. How much could anyone know about a thing like this.

I held my head in my hands, pressing hard against my temples, trying to straighten it all out. There was so much—and so very little. But I wanted him to know it all, of course—there was nothing I wanted to hide.

"Any way you want to tell it," the lieutenant said. "Or do you want me to ask questions?"

"I can tell you, all right," I said. . . .

There's one in every crowd (I told the lieutenant), no matter where you go. A wise guy. Always ready with the smart crack, the dig, the little gimmick to get your goat. In a bunch of GI's, or in a bunch of ex-GI's, you'll always find him. In any bunch of guys, I guess.

Well, that was Bruce Carter—a big, bluff, easy-to-know character who'd come back to college with the rest of us after the war. I'd only known him slightly before; we'd both been on the track squad. He was a year below me though, and we never went around together much. But he'd gone into the service a year later than myself, so when we came back we were both in the same junior class, and he and I and Spencer Grail were roomed together.

There were times when Bruce wasn't easy to take—he was hepped up on the war, and he kept referring to it every chance he got—but he didn't bother me as much as he bothered Spencer, who was kind of a quiet kid who didn't take to any kind of ribbing or riding.

Spence and Bruce, strangely enough, had both been in the 82nd Airborne Division—though they'd never met during the war, and with Spencer it wasn't a badge of distinction he had to carry back to school with him. As a matter of fact, Spencer had had a pretty tough time of it with the troopers, getting banged up in the Normandy show, after which he went through a succession of hospitals before he finally drew a medical discharge here in the States.

He ignored Bruce as much as possible, and though he'd sometimes pal around with me, Spence tried to stay pretty much by himself, it seemed. Naturally, a guy like Bruce kept after him.

It wasn't anything you could put your finger on, exactly. A question here, a crack there—but if you knew Spencer as well as I got to know him, you could see how his thin, white face would redden, and how he tightened up inside when Bruce tried opening him up on his war experiences.

Sometimes it was about girls. Bruce had another word for them, mostly; and he liked to get coarse about the subject. . . . Sometimes it was about combat. Admittedly the 82nd had had its share of battle, but to hear Bruce talk there hadn't been another outfit overseas.

He was going on about it at length one night and Spence, his face white with rage, screamed, "Shut up about it, damn you! It's over, now. It's over!" and stormed out of the room.

Bruce just smiled at the door. "Can you beat it! That Joe's just chirping for the birds!"

I said, "Why don't you leave him alone? He's still not over it, Bruce. The kid's upset about the deal the war gave him."

"He's got to face it," Bruce told me. "Hell, I'm doing him a favor. Talk him out of his dammed psychoneurosis."

LATER on that night I met Spencer down in the Long Bar, the place where we did our off-campus drinking. He was nursing a beer and looking badly shaken up. We had a couple and he told me that he was going to try to change his room in order to avoid Bruce.

"I just wanted you to know, Mort," he told me. "I wish you and I could still be roomies. But I can't take Bruce."

"Sure, kid," I said. "Sure."

So we had another, there in the booth, and Spence began to look better. Then Bruce put in unwelcome appearance. He came over and set three fresh beers on our table.

"Where the hell've you guys been? Here all the time? Why didn't you tell me you were coming down?"

I tried a laugh. "I though you'd be out rushing some chippie, wolf." And that wasn't smart on my part!

Bruce sat down, sliding Spencer back into the booth. "Had it all lined up, then figured the hell with it. Whatta these broads know? Bunch of kids." He dug Spencer with an elbow. "Not like the fillies over there, eh?" He pulled at his beer and slapped the table with a broad palm. "I should have gone to school at Heidelberg." He kissed his fingers into the air above the booth.

I saw Spencer start to fidget. He took a deep breath and pushed his hands against the table.

"Boy, those Heinies know the score," said Bruce. "They had the right approach." He chuckled. "Remember them in Normandy, Spence? You were still in the division then, weren't you?"

"Yes," Spencer said deliberately, desperately.

"Around St. Lo. The Jerries brought their women right along with them. Kept them in their foxholes." Bruce shook his head from side to side. "Now, that's the way to fight a war, man!"

Bruce finished his drink and ordered another round. He smacked his lips. "Boy, were those Jerries sore when we took those foxhole babes away from them!" His face showed that he was savouring the memory.

"Hurray for the paratroops," I said as

scornfully as possible to deflate him.

The scorn was lost on him. "You and your damned Air Corps!" He snorted. "All you guys had was a joy ride. Drop up in the wrong place and chase back to England. What a racket. You didn't even know there was a war on, not you fellows."

Spencer started to rise. "If you don't mind," he began.

"Me, too," I said to no one in particular. "I think it's time for us two to hit the sack."

"Clean beds, good chow," Bruce said thickly. "No trouble at all. Just a little flak now and then. While we played ring around the rosie with their 88's and burp guns. Mort, I bet you never saw a Jerry all through the war. Not like me and Spence, here. Tell him about those prisoners, Spence."

I could see that Bruce was feeling his drinks, but his mood was not mellow; it was maudlin. "No damn prisoners, said Headquarters. Only don't tell the folks back home. Just take 'em and shoot 'em in a field somewhere, get rid of them quickly. . . ."

I stole a quick glance at Spencer, and I didn't like what I saw. This was going beyond all good sense and good taste, this mood of Bruce's, and I wished to hell that he'd shut up. There was little you could say in the face of his mutterings.

"Maybe you think that's something, huh?" he demanded. "Hell, we had guys going off their nuts all the time. Killers! Legal little War Department killers! I heard we had one in the division who finally went out and started to kill them with his bare hands! Ain't that right, Spence?"

He laughed slowly, in disgust. "The Air Corps! Why, this guy used to grab them Jerries in his mitts and tear them apart. Did you ever see any of those

(Please continue on page 98)

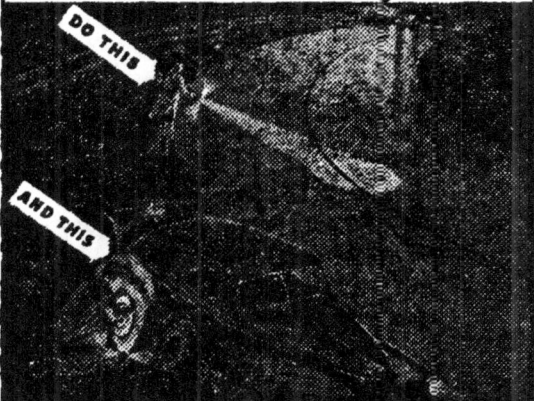

DOWNBEAT DIRGE

Spine-Chilling Novelette of Mad Music and Murder

By Robert Turner

Max Mercer's hot trumpet twisted the souls of a jitterbug, a glamour girl, a kootch dancer, and a girl who should have known better. . . . They'll tell you the shocking drama of this personable devil and his hellish horn.

Screaming, they watched Alec come leaping on top of me. . . .

PART ONE

*T*HE FOLLOWING *statements by Jennie Lee, jazz-crazy roadhouse kid, have been changed and reconstructed only enough to give coherence and sequence to her sometimes hysterical outbursts. This is, in her own words, what happened the night of March 21,*

31

1947 in the affair of herself and Max Mercer, the trumpet player. . . .

They ought to close that hell-hole up, that damned jimjam joint called the Jackpot. You've seen it; you know where I mean. Big place, set well back of the road on Route Seven, out of town. Shimmying neons outside, and inside, smoke you could cut through and semi-darkness and that throbbing, weird New Orleans style jazz that'll drive you crazy —if the rotgut liquor doesn't do it, first.

It wasn't only me, either. I could tell you things about the Jackpot that would curl your hair. The old rumbum who runs it doesn't care what happens there, so long as it puts a buck into his pocket. I mean plenty kids have gotten into trouble there, nice guys and gals that come from good families in town. All right, me, the odds were for me hanging out in a joint like that anyway. My old lady dead since I was ten; the old man away all the time, following the horses around the country. Me quitting school and out working for a living since I was fourteen. It was in the books for me.

The Jackpot is a lot to blame for this— and not having any decent place in town for kids to go and have their fun. If it wasn't for the Jackpot, I'd have never met Max Mercer, nor got that mad, hellish horn music of his so deep inside of me. It's worse than dope or alky.

If the Jackpot had been a decent place, Max Mercer wouldn't have been there playing. Max doesn't play any places except dives, any more. You know about him. The greatest hot horn man this country has ever known. Played with every name band in the biz, at one time or another. Lot of his early recordings are already collector's items. You ever hear Maxie play *Everybody Loves My Baby* or *Sugar Blues*? It knocks you out.

But you know why Max only plays in wingding joints anymore? Because no right place will have him. Because he's a mean, moody, vicious, egotistical heel that women go crazy over just because of that —or maybe because of the things he can do with that horn. Anyhow, wherever Max plays there's trouble—really low-down trouble, before long.

You've seen him, his picture anyhow. What is it that gets them? He's not good looking, not in the ordinary way. Too thin and all bones in his face, and those brown, sad, mean, haunting eyes sunk way in and skin the color of muta paper—not just plain pale, like most musicians. And that wavy, funny-color brown hair that looks like its never been combed.

That kind of hot, wild, off-beat jazz wasn't new to me. I'd heard it before. But not the way it was when Max Mercer got in on it with that beat-up old horn of his. It wasn't just the trumpet genius of Max, himself. Any outfit he played with was suddenly inspired. They blew their wings and made music madness like it had never been made before.

I went to the Jackpot, that first night I saw Max, with a nice kid I'd been going with fairly steady. He was a good kid, quiet and serious, who never drank too much. But that was the last I saw of him. After I heard Max and that band, I didn't look at my escort another time. It got late and the boy friend kept after me to let's get out of there and go home, but I didn't even hear him for a long while and when I did I cussed him out and told him to leave me alone.

That's the way Max and his music hit me the first time. I went there every night after that. If I had the dough, I took a cab from town and went out there alone. That was the way I liked it best, just to be by myself and listen to Max play and watch him. But when I was broke, I'd get somebody—anybody—to take me out there. I'd do anything to get to go out there to that damned Jackpot place. Monday nights when the band was off I like to went crazy.

FOR the first couple of weeks Max didn't even know I was alive, I guess. And that was all right, at first. Just so I could sit there and watch him and listen to him. You don't know what it did to me when that guy took off on a hot riff. It broke me up. I'd get to trembling and sort of feverish restless so that I could hardly sit still. And I could feel the blood rushing and roaring through my veins, pumping and pounding the pulses in my wrists and temples until they caught up with the mad beat of the music. You don't know what it was like, I tell you.

You know how too many martinis hype you up sometime? Well, with Max and that wild horn of his, it was like that a thousand times over. It was like when someone you're nuts about kisses you for the first time full on the mouth. Only it stayed like that, every minute I could see Max and hear him play. And after awhile it got so that I could even see him and hear him in my sleep.

I guess it was seeing me in the same booth alongside the dance floor every night for so long that attracted his attention. Anyhow, one night, in a break between sets, on his way out to the bar, he looked right at me as he passed the booth and gave a quick little grin.

"You here again tonight, baby?" he said. "You must be glued to that booth."

That was all. But it made me dizzy and that crazy, dim roadhouse room reeled and swam around and I almost fainted. Two or three nights, then, after that, he spoke on his way out to the bar. Then he stopped cold by that booth—and so did my heart.

"Chick," he said with that crazy, crooked little grin of his, "you look knocked out. You need some joy-juice but fast. Come on out to the bar with me and have your pleasure."

I don't know how I made it out there. I was scuffing through clouds all the way. I was floating. I was going up in

smoke. All at the same time. We had some drinks and he got my name and introduced me to the other guys in the band, but I didn't hear their names or see their faces. I couldn't get my eyes off of Max Mercer. I kept looking at that lip of his and the thin down of mustache he always left on it, like a lot of horn men do; because if they ever slip in their shaving and cut that upper lip and maybe injure one of the sensitive nerves or muscles, they're through. A horn man is as good as his lip and that's all. That lip was perfectly matched with the lower one, not too thin and not too wide but strong and mobile looking.

I kept thinking of the things that mouth could do with a horn. I thought about the things those lips could do to me if I ever got to kiss them. . . .

Tonight? Okay, I tell you, I'm getting to tonight, but this is all part of it.

It went on from there. After the drinks Max told me if I wanted to wait around, he would ride me home. Okay, I waited. And from then on I waited every night until the Jackpot closed. Sometimes we'd go to one of the private dining rooms upstairs and split a fried chicken between us—Max was always hungry after a night of knocking himself out on that horn—and talk and maybe drink some more. Or maybe we'd just ride, or park somewhere until almost daylight.

None of that was doing me any good. I had a job daytimes. I wasn't getting any sleep hardly, and I lost weight. The way I felt about Max was like a sickness almost; he was like a fever in me all the time. I smoked too much and drank too much and that didn't help any, either.

It lasted about ten days. Then one night Max didn't stop by my booth on his way out for a drink. He went another way. He sent a note over by a waiter, saying I'd better not wait around until closing that night because he was going somewhere with the guys in the band for an after-hours jive session with them.

That first night, I didn't think much about it. But the next night it started to get me. He didn't want me to wait around because he had a recording session on the next A.M. and he wanted to get some sleep. The third night, he didn't bother making any excuse at all. He just let me wait around. When the place closed down I saw that there was another girl waiting there. She wasn't a girl, really—she was a good ten years older than I.

She's married, this Ina Courtney. Deems Courtney's wife—he's one of the richest old guys in town. And Ina is plenty wild, too. The things I could tell you about her. . . . That—that's where you'll find him, now! With her! I know it. I—I can feel it, I tell you. He's gone to her, to that stinking rich, blonde, hip-switching no-good little—

At this point, Jennie Lee's account became an almost insane, incoherent babbling, but in a few minutes she suddenly came out of this momentary frenzy of hatred and jealousy and went on almost normally.

That first night I saw him take Ina home instead of me, I pleaded with him to tell me what I'd done, why he was through with me, He just let those deep-set, weird-looking brown eyes, full of moods and mystery, go over me sort of slow and the corner of his mouth curled. He said:

"Baby, you got a hide thick enough to make into drum skins. You don't take a hint very well, do you, sugar? Why don't you smarten up? You were a cute little chicken dinner but a guy needs a change of diet. Buzz off, baby! Take your feet and make 'em scuff!"

I STOOD there like somebody had clubbed me in the jaw with a bung-starter. I watched them walk away. I was sick, really sick, all that night and the next day; I didn't even go to work. I didn't go out to the Jackpot that night, either. I had some pride, at first. But then the fever that was Max Mercer began to eat at me and there was no more pride, no more nothing but this yen and yearning to see Max just once more, to hear that wonderful, thrill-you-through horn music of his.

I started going out there again and just sitting there, getting drunk and looking at him and listening to him and leaving just before closing-up time. That went on for a week and all that time Max Mercer never let on that he knew I was alive. Ina Courtney was there every night, too.

Then, tonight, something happened. I don't know. Maybe it was the liquor and the music finally got me. But I think it was just suddenly that I had to show Max what he did to me, that everything that he and his music meant to me had been bottled up inside of me too long and it had to come out someway.

Anyhow, the band was playing this terrific *Weak and Willing Blues* and Max was taking the break and tearing down the roof with an off-the-elbow solo on his horn. Nobody was dancing. The half-dozen couples that were there that late were just huddled around the bandstand, watching and listening to him, all jittered up.

All of a sudden that horn started to hurt my ear drums. It seemed to go all through me and split every nerve end to frazzles. I got up out of the booth, screaming once, high and keen as Max on a high note, and walked, stiff-limbed, like a sleep walker, out onto the dance floor.

Then I started to dance, all by myself, in time to the music. I guess you'd call it a dance, yet it wasn't any step I'd ever done before, nothing that they ever teach you in dancing school. It wasn't any ball-room stuff. I remember my feet didn't hardly move at all. It didn't even seem like me who was doing that dance. It was as though the music had gotten inside of me and was making me go through those motions.

You remember the Charleston and the Blackbottom—well, there was some of those steps in this that I was doing and I guess some of every other dance of that type that was ever invented—plus a few little ideas of my own.

I couldn't tell you, but it must have been something to see. The other couples and the band—after it was over—shrieked and whistled and stomped, fit to knock down the walls. They wanted more. But I was through. As soon as the music stopped, it was as though all the blood was let out of my veins. Somehow I got back to the booth and fell into it and went to sobbing.

The next thing I knew, Max Mercer was standing beside me and shaking my shoulder. He was saying: "What the hell's the matter with you, you screwball little chippie?"

I looked up at him, glassy-eyed with tears and something else. I kept saying: "I—I couldn't help it, Max. I couldn't help it. At—least, it made you come and talk to me."

"You got to quit this!" he said. "You got to stay away from here from now on. You want to get this place closed up?"

It took a minute for that to sink in. Then I reached out and grabbed his hand and he pulled it roughly away when my nails started to dig in. I'd gotten this idea. I cried:

"Max, you want to get rid of me? Let me wait for you, tonight. Take—take me home just once more, tonight, Max and I swear, if you say so, I'll never bother you again. I'll never come here; you'll never see me again."

He thought about that and my heart was up in my throat beating there and choking me, because I knew if I could be alone with him just this one more time, I'd make him feel the same about me

as I did about him. I'd make everything the way it was before.

"Okay," he said finally. And I kept on crying, only it was with happiness now.

I don't know how he got rid of Ina Courtney. I didn't care. Anyhow, she left. When the Jackpot closed up, I went out with Max and got into that battered old roadster. I told him: "You can't drive me home. Take me out to Lover's Paradise, Max. Just for a little while. I've got to talk to you and it's got to be there."

IT DID, too. That was the place Max and I always used to go when we didn't go straight home. There was something about that place, high up on that cliff, overlooking the valley and the town in the distance. It wasn't only the loneliness; there was something about the atmosphere of the spot that fitted right in with your mood, after listening to that wild music all night and being in love with a no-good hell of a jazz genius that you knew would never truly do you any good.

Max cussed a little, but turned down the road that leads to that wide flat of rock on the edge of the bluff. He parked in the usual place. Then I told him how I felt, how sick and crazy I'd been since he'd thrown me over and that if he'd only take me back I'd do anything in the world for him, steal or kill or anything He listened to me and when I was all through, he just stared, hard-eyed and said:

"You should have seen yourself, out there on that dance floor, like some dam', cheap, crazy little kootch dancer!" His eyes got a funny, faraway look in them when he said that. It was strange. And his features got all tight and red around the cheekbones and he got very angry looking. He kept saying it over: "Like a little kootch dancer!"

Even that didn't stop me, though, and I kept after him. I pleaded and begged and kissed his hand and when he yanked it away, I tried to throw myself into his arms. I told him that he had to take me back.

That was when he laughed. That was when he told me that *he* didn't *have* to do anything and he wouldn't take me back if I was draped in diamonds and owned the mint at Fort Knox. And all the time he laughed. Not just plain laughing, but the kind of sound someone makes when they're watching another person make a complete fool of themselves. He said I ought to stop talking and acting like a little kid.

Well, Max was a good fifteen years older than I, at least. About thirty-five, I guess he was and my being so much younger was always a sore spot with me. Max was so wise and had been around so much, I often felt like a baby, but he'd never rubbed that in before. That and the laughing did it. I got out of the car. I don't know where I was going or why. I didn't care. I just suddenly had to get away from him. And I had to hurt him just a little before I left. I called back over my shoulder:

"You're right. I am just a kid, compared to you. I don't know why I ever had anything to do with an old fogie, old enough to be my father. You—you got your nerve, playin' around with girls my age and wise-crackin' and cuttin' up as though *you* were really young, too!"

It was crazy the way that hit him. He went red with rage. He jumped out of the car and came tearing after me, swearing. He grabbed me and swung me around and yelled: "Don't you ever say anything like that about my age!" Wasn't that a whacky thing for him to say?

Then he hit me. He slapped me back and forth across the face, harder than I'd ever even been slapped by my old man, making my ears ring and ache. I started to cry. And then I—I realized that we were on the edge of the cliff. He was wrestling me around. I suddenly—*realized!* I screamed:

"No—Max! . . . Don't throw me over! Max! . . ."

I grabbed at him, but when I started to go over, my hand slipped away and all that I held onto was a leather button from his sport jacket. I got it clenched here in my hand right now. That'll hang him.

I saw the moon and the stars go rolling lazily, like a slow motion picture, around my head. I saw a nighthawk, wheeling high above me. I remembered that the cliff was several hundred feet high and there was nothing but huge, jagged rocks at the bottom. The sound of my own screaming almost split my ear-drums. . . .

PART TWO

*T*HE FOLLOWING *is the statement of Ina Mae Courtney, glamorous blonde young society matron, dealing with the murder of her husband, Deems H. Courtney and other events of the night of March 21, 1947. . . .*

I had known Max Mercer about two weeks. Please don't get the idea that I'm one of these jazz babies. I can't stand what is commonly called popular music. It grates on my nerves. But I'd heard a lot about this place called the Jackpot and about this wild and woolly music they put out there. So one night, hoping a visit there might take the edge off of my boredom, I paid the place a visit.

It turned out to be a dirty, smoky, depressing dive and I wouldn't have stayed ten minutes. But right after our party entered, the trumpet player in the band stood up to take a solo. Even though I don't care for that sort of thing, ordinarily, there was something compelling in the music that came out of this man's horn.

There was an unrestrained wildness to it that attracted me. It gave me a delicious sort of shivery feeling and stirred up a rebellion against convention that had been simmering deep inside of me for a long, long time.

A few minutes later, when the band played a slower number for dancing, my partner maneuvered close to the bandstand. Looking over my partner's shoulder, I was aware of the eyes of this trumpet man fixed upon me.

I suppose he had something to stare at. Our whole party—a girl friend of mine, her husband and her rather stupid young brother—was a little overdressed for the Jackpot. We'd come from a dull dance at the country club that my husband had insisted I go to, even though he couldn't make it. The men were in white tie and tails. Carlotta and I were wearing evening gowns. Mine was a new one that Deems, my husband, had clucked his tongue over and tabbed a little on the daring side. I didn't look at it that way. It was completely decent, although it did, with its clinging black velvet, accentuate the lines of my figure. But what's wrong with a young woman attractively displaying the curves which nature gave to her?

But perhaps this particular gown was a little on the bold side, because this trumpet player couldn't seem to take his eyes away from me. It was the most peculiar sensation. At first it made me uncomfortable but then I was aware of a tingling warmth, as on a hot summer day, when you run out onto the beach for the first few moments in scanty swimming attire and the sun's rays strike your flesh.

Well, one thing led to another and I found myself talking our group into staying at this roadhouse a little longer. Then I was out at the bar. At the time it seemed that it was completely unpremeditated, accidental, but later I often wondered if one of us—or both—hadn't worked it that way deliberately.

Out at the bar I looked around suddenly —and this trumpet player, Max Mercer, was standing next to me. There was no one else right near us.

He smiled—if you'd call it that. It was the most knowing and bold expression I'd ever seen on a man's face. He said, so softly I could hardly hear:

"What makes you think you're so hot, honey? What makes you raise that cute little nose so high and snooty as though you smelled something bad in here? Those jewels and expensive clothes don't fool Maxie. You're just a little floozy under that, like any other dame."

He caught me by surprise. What do you say to a man who speaks to you that way for the first time? After all, I came from one of the oldest families in South City. I was Mrs. Deems Courtney, rich and respected. Two-bit musicians in run-down road houses didn't speak to me that way and get away with it.

But Max Mercer did. I somehow instinctively knew that it was no use trying to fool him, that he'd sized me up right. For a moment I was stunned, and then I laughed and said: "At least you're refreshing. Have a drink with me?"

That was how it started. I went out to the Jackpot the next night, alone. Max came over and we talked and he asked if I'd give him a date after the place closed up. He said that there was another girl—and I saw her glowering at us from a booth on the other side of the room. She was a pretty little thing in a dark, wild-eyed and pale sort of way. He said he could handle her, get rid of her all right. So I told him it was a date.

I saw Max Mercer regularly after that. He was something new to me. He wasn't afraid of me or my name or background, or the fact that I was Deems Courtney's wife, like a lot of young men I'd had dates with from time to time.

In fact, he seemed to get a boot out of it. I'll say one thing for Max and let it go at that. There was never a dull moment with him. Believe me, that's saying a lot for me. I thought I'd known every kind of man there was to know. I thought I'd heard it all and done it all. But there were times when Max Mercer made me feel like a school child.

It was after I'd known him a week or so that I began to think about—doing away with my husband. You've got to understand how it was, with Deems and I. I had never loved him. He was a good thirty years older than I. We'd been married for ten years and the sophistication and gray hairs that had fascinated me at first finally bored hell out of me. You see, in a lot of ways, there was more than the difference in age between Deems and me.

Then there was his drinking. The past few years, he was rarely sober. By the time of evening other couples were ready to go out somewhere, Deems was tight as a coot and ready to pass out. I'm not

alibiing. I'm just saying the way it was, take it or leave it.

BUT the worst thing of all was the way he was getting cagey with his money. He kept the purse strings tied tightly and he was clever about it. I had enough money to keep up appearances, but when there's over a million in the bank, it galls a woman not to have unlimited use of it. And lately, Deems had been objecting to what he called my "gallivanting around."

I don't think he knew about Max or the Jackpot. But he knew something was going on. And one night when he was very drunk, he told me that he'd fix things so that I wouldn't get a cent of his money after he died, if I didn't calm down and stay home nights. We had a big fight about that and it got me to thinking.

Well, this night, all the vague, half-formed plans I'd been nursing lately about getting rid of Deems—suddenly crystalized. The one thing that had always stopped me was how to do Deems in, without getting into any trouble myself. I knew that murder was a difficult thing to get away with. But tonight I was suddenly presented with the answer to that problem.

I was at the Jackpot, as usual, killing time, drinking and listening to the music, when out of a blue sky, this little ex-girl friend of Max's, this wild-looking kid named Jennie Lee, suddenly went berserk from the liquor or the music or both and trotted out onto the dance floor and performed this wierd, exhibitionistic dance.

I saw that Max got all upset about this. I saw him go over and talk to her, after it was all over. Then he came to me and told me that he had to skip our date tonight, that he had to see this kid and get rid of her for all time. He was afraid that maybe she might cause some serious trouble if she kept hanging around there, and might, as Max put it, "blow her buttons" and do something really awful.

I said that was okay and I left. That is, I left the Jackpot, but I didn't go home. I got into my car and pulled off the road into the shadow of a grove of big trees within sight of the road house and waited there. I was going to follow him and this girl. There were several reasons, all mixed in together. Maybe I was a little jealous. Maybe I was just curious as to how he would act with some other woman. I never bothered to analyze my motives. Perhaps I had an intuition that there would be trouble and that I could use it in some way.

Anyhow, an hour or so later, the neon lights of the Jackpot went off. Max and this kid, Jennie, came out and got into his car. I followed them to this well-known necking rendezvous, called Lover's Paradise.

I couldn't attempt to fully describe what happened there. In the first place, I couldn't hear what was being said between them, in the car. I had to park my coupe down the road and follow them to the bluff on foot. I was hiding behind a clump of shrubbery about ten or fifteen yards away from Max's car. I heard them having this terrific row, even though I couldn't hear the details. Then the girl jumped out of the car and shouted something at Max. He ran after her. They had some more words and then he hit her in the face with the flat of his hand, half a dozen times.

That had a strange effect on this girl. It didn't seem to make her angry. I'm sure that once I heard her pleading with him to hit her again. She said that showed that he really loved her. Then for a few minutes I couldn't hear what was said, but the next thing, Max was laughing wildly at her. This seemed to drive Jennie Lee into a frenzy and she attacked him, clawed at him, all the time sobbing and crying like the damned.

The next thing I saw, she wheeled away from him and ran toward the edge of the cliff. Just before she hurled herself over the edge, she yelled something like:

"I'll see you in hell, Max Mercer! We'll be there together, forever. I'm going first, but I'm going to drag you after me!"

And then she was gone and there was only the sound of her screaming for a moment, before she hit the bottom and it was cut off sharply. The silence that followed was horrible.

What's that? Of *course* it was exactly like that. That's the way it actually happened. There was a bright moon and I wasn't more than thirty feet away and saw the whole thing.

For a few minutes, Max stood there dazed and stunned and it was then that I got this other idea. I went to him. He was scared and in a sort of mental fog. It was easy to talk him into going home with me to have a drink and try to straighten himself out and figure what he should do about the death of Jennie Lee.

My husband, Deems, was out to his lodge meeting, so I knew it would be all right to take Max home. It took half a dozen shots to get Max to the point where he stopped shaking and was able to think and talk coherently. Then I went to work on him.

"Max, darling," I said, "do you realize that nobody knows what happened out there on that cliff, tonight, except you and me? Do you realize what a spot you're in?"

"Sure," he said. He blinked at me, heavy-lidded and exhausted. "It was a good thing for me you followed and saw everything, or I might have trouble convincing the cops that I didn't kill that crazy kid. I—"

"You certainly would, Max," I cut in. "Look at you, with your jacket ripped and one of the buttons torn off. Imagine what would happen, Max, if I denied that I was there and saw what happened?

. . . Or if I swore it was the other way, testified that you had deliberately pushed Jennie off that cliff, murdered her!"

HE GOT green around the mouth. His eyes almost popped out. Then he laughed a little weakly. "Don't kid like that, Ina," he said. "For a moment, you had me scared!"

I told him: "You have nothing to be frightened about. You won't ever have to worry about me doing anything like that. . . . Provided you act sensible—and do a few favors for me."

For a moment he didn't seem to understand. Then his eyes narrowed and he stared at me long and hard. Finally, he said: "'Just what are you getting at, Ina?"

There was no sense in beating around the bush. I gave it to him straight. Even as I talked about it, so coldly, so easily, once I started, I began to get all excited. It was so simple; such a perfect plan.

"You're going to help me kill my husband tonight, Max," I told him. "It will be simple. There will be no danger, if we don't get nervous or lose our heads. If we work together. We—"

He jumped up. "What are you talking about?" he demanded. "Are you out of your mind?" He rubbed his hand over his deeply sunken eyes, over his pale and haggard face. He started toward the door. "I'm getting out of here, Ina. Two stark, raving crazy dames in one night is too much for me."

I didn't get excited. Softly, I said: "Max, the instant you go out that door, I'll call the police about Jennie Lee. I'll tell them I *saw* you kill her. They'll believe my word against yours. All the evidence is against you."

I saw him stop stiff and still and his long, lean fingers kept opening and clenching against his thighs. I said: "Come back and sit down and let's talk this over sensibly, Max. If I keep quiet, you are in no danger. Nobody will ever have to know you were with Jennie Lee tonight."

Slowly, he turned and went over and fell into a chair. He sat there with his elbows on his knees, his face between his hands and listened while I told him what we were going to do.

My husband, Deems, always came home from his lodge meeting dead drunk. When Deems got that way it always went to his legs badly. He was awkward and clumsy and always falling. Only a few months ago, he'd had a bad fall on the stairs and had to be treated by our family physician for a lacerated skull and bruises and contusions.

"Tonight, Max," I finished, "when Deems comes home, you are going to be hiding behind the door. As he starts up the stairs, you are going to hit him over the head. We will then place his body in a position so that it will look as though he fell down the stairs. Only this time, fatally!"

I had a lot of trouble talking Max into it. He was afraid. I had to use every trick in the book. I had to threaten and cajole. I promised that later, he and I would go away together somewhere and that he wouldn't ever have to work or worry about money again. I told him that even though he hadn't actually killed Jennie Lee, he was directly responsible for her death. What difference would another violent death make? He finally gave in.

While we were waiting for Deems to come home—was a very bad time for both of us. Perspiration poured off of Max's thin, tired face in little rivers, soaked his collar. He kept looking at the club-like small log of firewood about which I'd wrapped a piece of heavy black velvet, so that there would be no unnecessary bleeding from the blow to Deems' head. Afterward, we would burn both the log and the velvet in the fireplace, where a fire was already roaring.

I kept watching Max, the nervous twining of his fingers, the way he smoked half a pack of cigarettes in deep, long, frantic drags. My own nerves were strung tight as fiddle strings. I thought Deems would never get home.

Then we both jumped as he heard the limousine pull up and stop under the *porte cochiere*. I saw Max bend and pick up the murder weapon. I motioned him to his place behind the door. I heard the car door slam, outside, and Deems' rasping, drunken voice, as he dismissed the chauffeur for the evening. And then I ran to the top of the stairs, to carry out our plan, as Deems came lurching through the front door.

I looked down there at him and I felt no pity, only a sort of loathing for this fat, drunken sot, with his gray and balding head, with his red face and bleared eyes, with the baggy purple pouches under them. I looked at the dewlaps of veined flesh at his jaws, like turkey wattles. A strange exultation swept me to think that soon I would be rid of this stupid old oaf, that soon now, all his money would be mine and that I wouldn't ever have to look at him or listen to him, or escape from him on the sly ever again.

I called down the stairs: "Deems, angel, will you come right upstairs, please! Right away. Something's happened!"

He stood there, swaying, blinking up at me, owlishly. "Sure. Sure, honey," he said thickly. "Wha's matter up there?"

He started stumbling, holding onto the bannister, up the steps. I waited for Max to come out of his hiding place and strike. He didn't come and I got panicky. He couldn't let me down now. We had to go through with it. I yelled:

"Max! *Now,* Max! Hurry!"

THAT did it. Max ran out from behind the door. He raised the black velvet-covered club of wood over his head. The expression on his face was a terrible thing to see, all loathing and fear and guilt. Just before he struck, he closed his eyes in some kind of reflex fear. And at the same instant, Deems, drunk as he was, became warned by my outcry and half turned.

Max's blow did not hit Deems squarely across the back of the head. It struck, but only a glancing blow. Deems fell against the bannister and then his fingers slipped off and he went down. He tumbled down the three steps to the bottom, moved once, feebly and lay still.

I could tell by the way he had fallen that the blow had not been hard enough. It had not killed him. It had only knocked him unconscious. I yelled:

"Max! Hit him again! Finish him off, Max. You've got to. We must go through with it now! He knows!"

Max Mercer stood there, holding onto the bannister, flattened back against it, where he'd swung out of the way to let Deems' body fall past him. He held the club loosely at his side. He was breathing noisily, his lips pulled back from his teeth. He kept staring down at the limp, twisted figure of my husband. He said, hoarsely:

"I can't, Ina. . . . I feel as though I'm goin' to be sick. My Lord, Ina, I *can't* do it again. I *won't!*"

I waited for a moment that seemed like eternity. Then panic struck me. There was no telling how long Deems would remain unconscious. Once he came to, we were licked. The job had to be finished. I could see that Max was scared silly. Reaction had hit him and I doubted if he had the strength any more to even lift that club.

I raced down the stairs, swearing at Max. I reached down and snatched the club out of his hand. "You stupid, blundering lout!" I screamed at him. "*I'll* do it! I should have done it, myself, in the first place!"

Past him, I moved, to the foot of the

stairs. I bent over Deems' still figure and raised the club to deliver the final killing blow to the back of his skull. But I never did swing it. Max Mercer jumped down the stairs and grabbed at my upraised arm. He was wild-eyed. He said:

"Stop it, Ina! Put that down. You can't go through with this crazy idea. We'll both hang for it!"

In a fit of temper and frustration, I twisted free from his grip and swung the club at him. The blow caught Max across the top of the forehead, a solid, smashing blow. He fell on his face. I ignored him and turned to Deems again and finished the job with him. That was how my husband was murdered. . . .

After it was done, I stood there for I don't know how long, looking down at both of them. Max had his face turned up to me and he was white as cotton batting, but one eyelid was twitching and the corner of his mouth. I knew he was still alive. I tried to figure what to do with him but suddenly I couldn't seem to figure anything clearly anymore. I became emotionally numbed, now that it was all over.

Before I snapped out of it, Max moaned and swung over onto his stomach. Slowly, he got up onto all fours. Then he grabbed hold of the balustrade and pulled himself erect. He stood there, swaying and blinking, with his hand to his forehead, the fingertips tenderly feeling of the black and blue lump.

Fnally he turned toward me and he started. His eyes had a vague, foggy look in them. And it was a strange thing, but Max suddenly looked different. I don't know how to rightly explain it. It was just that—well, the expression on his face had changed some. Some of the hard look was gone from it. And he looked *younger, less mature!*

"What are we going to do now, Max?" I whispered.

He stared at me. He shook his head groggily. He said: "Wh-who are you?"

I frowned. "Max," I said, "don't you know me?"

"Max?" he repeated the name in a sort of numbed tone of voice. "Who's Max? *My* name isn't Max, lady."

It took a moment for it to sink in and even then, right away, I wasn't sure whether he was trying to kid me. I knew that a hard blow to the head like I had given Max had been known to produce amnesia.

"Max," I said softly, "Don't you remember—anything?"

HE LOOKED scared, a peculiar, boyish fright, like you might see on the face of a kid in a graveyard late at night. He glanced around at the rich and lavish furnishings of the hall, as though he'd never seen them before. Then his frightened eyes cut back to me.

"Stop calling me Max, lady!" he said. "That's not my name. I'm Alec Sherman." He put his fingertips to the lump on his forehead again, winced and swayed a little. "My head hurts," he complained. "Listen, I—I'd better get home. The old man will skin me alive. He sent me out for a bottle o' liquor and I stopped to watch a gang o' kids playin' one-o-cat.

"I had to run, then, to make up time, so I wouldn't be gone too long. I wasn't lookin' where I was goin', crossin' the street. I guess that's how come I got hit by that car." He looked around him, again.

"Where am I, lady? It—it was real nice for you to take me in, but I'm all right, now. I got to get Pop's liquor and get it back to the Carny. Which way is it from here, lady?"

"Carny?" I said. I didn't know what he was talking about. Something had happened to Max Mercer's brain with that blow on the skull. I was sure of that, now. He wasn't fooling, I could see.

"Yeah," he said. "You know, the tent

show out on State Street. My—my old man and I work there. He's a barker."

"You say you are Alec Sherman?" I stopped him. "And you don't know me, never saw me before in your life?" Listening to him, as though maybe he was delirious or out of his head, gave me the chills. Because there was no carnival anywhere around this part of the country. There was no State Street in any town nearby.

He shook his head doggedly. Then I pointed to the sprawled, twisted, dead figure of my husband, on the floor, a little to the left and behind Max. I said: "What about him? Do you know him?" Perhaps this was going to work out all right, after all.

He half turned and sort of jumped. He gulped and stared down at the dead man on the floor. "No. No, ma'am," he said positively. "What happened to him?"

I took a deep breath. "You ought to know that," I said. "I don't know what kind of an act you're trying to pull here. You're a burglar. You broke into our house, and my husband caught you. There was a struggle and you—you killed him."

He put his hand to his forehead again. His eyes widened and one corner of his lips began to twitch and perspiration began to bead on his forehead.

"No!" he said. "I—I don't understand. That—that auto hit me and everything went black on me. Now I come to here and you say—"

"You'd better get out of here," I told him. "The police are coming."

He shook his head wildly. "The police!" he repeated agonizingly. "I can't get mixed up with no cops. The ol' man, he'd wallop the tar out of me!"

He suddenly twitched all over and spun on his heel and made a mad dash toward the door. He had trouble getting it open. He was all thumbs. But then he made it and the door slammed shut again after

him and he was gone. I let him go. I figured that I could call the police and give his description and he would be picked up in an hour or so.

But it didn't work out that way. I never saw Max Mercer—or Alec Sherman, as he called himself—ever again. . . .

PART THREE

*T*HIS IS *the report from Nate Sherman, one-time circus roustabout, carnival barker and finally owner of the Big-Little Tent Show, at his bedside in the accident ward of the Heightstown City Hospital.* . .

What you tell me is hard to take. I've seen some crazy things and heard crazier, battin' around in circuses and penny-peep shows and fly-by-night town-hop carnies all my life. But this beats all. Telling me you think that goon of a stepson of mine is really Max Mercer, the world's greatest jazz trumpet player. It don't make sense. But what does, in this cockeyed world?

All I say, is, I hope you're right. I'll bleed him for every cent he's got. Why? You listen and I'll tell you why. The trouble that kid and his no-good, two-timin' mother have caused me in my life. . .

Leah worked in a can-can girlie show in Tallman's Traveling Circus when I first met her. She was the most beautiful dam' female you ever set your eyes on, with long, soft brown hair and with the sweet face of an angel. And what a figure —say, listen, if she'd had a brain to back up that beauty, Leah wouldn't have wasted her time in any rotten little sideshow. She could have been a big musical comedy star. But she wasn't only no'count, she was stupid. But still I went nuts over her. I guess I wasn't so bright at the time, either.

Anyhow, she had this kid, by a former husband, a roustabout, who ran off and left her flat after they'd been married about a month. She had a tough time, I figger, bringin' that brat up, all by herself, hoppin' from town to town with the shows. The carny business was the only thing she knew. Later, I got it figgered that's the only reason she married me—to get some support for the kid.

Well, we were happy for awhile. But after about a year, she met this guy who joined the show with a kewpie doll concession. He was a young, slick, fast-talkin' John and all the gals in the show were goo-goo eyed over him right from the start. I got sick and laid up in the hospital shortly after that. When I came back, Leah was different, somehow. She was very cold to me and we fought all the time.

Then one night she disappeared. This kewpie doll guy was gone, too. They'd run off together. But she left the kid behind her. She left me stuck with him. I blew my top for sure, then. I went on a roaring drunk for about five days. I tried very way to catch up with Leah and this guy she run away with. If I'd made it, I'd've killed 'em both. I guess you might say it kind of made me a little nuts.

I calmed down some when I sobered up, but I didn't get over it. I took to broodin' all the time and I got mean and ugly. I drank all the time. And I decided to keep the kid. I could have put him in a home or somethin', but I had another idea. I was goin' to get my revenge on Leah, through her son.

You see, she had great plans for that kid, at first. One night, when I first knew her, she told me about them. He was going to be somebody. He was going to go to school and study. He wasn't going to grow up and just be any old carny barker or shill or concessionaire. She said she'd die before she'd let him work in a tent show.

Maybe this sounds kind of mean and —and brutal to you. Okay, it was that. So was what she had done to me. Any-

how, that was the only way I could get at her, get the burning, poisonous hate I had for her out of me. I took it out on that kid. After a few years it was easier to do because he started to show signs of lookin' like her. He had a lot of her cute little ways about him, too. He got to be more and more like her, the older he grew. And I got to hate him more.

I brought him up to wait on me hand and foot like a slave. I used to whale hell out of him. And I never let him get any learnin', either. Sometimes I had trouble with school authorities in some of these little spit-ant towns when some local biddie would see the kid hangin' around the girlie shows or listenin' to the roustabouts cuss. But mostly it was all right, because the show was moving all the time.

When he was ten, I decided to put him into show business just because I knew his mother wouldn't want it. We had a midget at that time, who played a cornet in front of the kootch show, to attract attention so's I could start my spiel. Well, the midget checked out on us one day, and there was nobody to take his place. That gave me an idea.

I dudded the kid up in cut down fancy-dog clothes of my own and hacked out and bought the cheapest cornet I could find in a hock shop. At first I just made him get up there and blow hell out of it, make a lot of noise to attract attention. But between shows I made him learn how to play it. I kept after him, with a razor strop and he learned fast how to toot that horn. He got to be pretty good for a kid.

His Maw must have born some of her hate for tent-show business right into him. Because he sure had it. Sometimes his inborn high-falutin' ideas irked me and I'd have to lay into him.

The girls in that kootch show were a tough bunch and they used to rag him a lot. He was always a kind of quiet, moody kid and I guess he made them feel uncomfortable or somethin'. They used to always tease him by tryin' to steal kisses or pinch him in the cheeks, stuff like that.

You know how show girls are. And the more emberrassed he'd get about the way they danced and went around between shows not so dressed up, the more they'd go out of their way to do some more of that. He got to hate kootch dancers and females in general, I guess. That was good. It suited me fine if he got to be mean as hell to women. It would be all right with me if he always hated the whole dam' female sex.

IT WENT on like that until he was about fifteen—when he ran away. I sent the little stinker into town for a bottle of *Old Tom* corn one afternoon and he never came back. I figgered he'd just got fed up and pulled stakes. . .

I sort of forgot about him, then. I guess, too, I'd worked most of my hate for Leah out onto him. Once he was gone, I straightened up a little. I worked hard and saved some moolah and—well, I've had my own show for the last ten years.

It was about three months ago—mind you, nearly twenty years since I'd seen that kid, Alec—that a crazy thing happened. A guy came into the office wagon of the show one morning when I was busy goin' over the books. I didn't feel so good, either, hung-over bad as I was.

He was a thin, weird-looking Joe, his cheeks sunken in, his face heavy with beard stubble. There was something disturbingly familiar about him, but I didn't grab it right away. He looked like a bum. He was wearing a sport jacket and slacks, but they were ripped and stained and rumpled. He smelled like a geek. He had a crazy, sort of half-vacant look on his face. He was carrying a small package in a paper sack. He handed it to me, sort of flinching. He said:

"There it is, Paw. I—I'm sorry I'm so late. . . ."

I looked at him as though he was nuts. I unwrapped the package and there was a bottle of *Old Tom* corn. It hit me all of a lump, then, who he was. "Alec!" I yelled, startled.

I got a little scared then. He was skinny as a rail, but large boned and taller than average. And you can't ever tell about these skinny, wiry guys; sometimes they can lick their weight in wildcats. Strong as steel rods, sometimes. And I thought this bringin' me the bottle o' corn was a gag or something. I was a little leery, too, that maybe he'd remembered all those beatings and come back to give me a goin' over. I was getting old and he could give me a hard time all right, if he wanted to.

"Good to see you, kid!" I said. "What brings you back to the tent shows?"

He just looked at me. Then a sort of relieved look came over his face and he sat down on the floor and started to boohoo. He cried like a baby. Like he used to do when I'd lam him good, back when he was a kid. I let him be. After awhile he quieted down to just plain sobbing and started to talk a little.

It was hard to understand most of what he said. There was a lot of stuff about watching a one-o-cat game and this car hittin' him and how he must've got lost or kidnaped, or something—and it took him a long time to get back. Then he looked up at me, his thin, whiskered face tear-streaked and with a kind of sad, dumb look and said:

"I'm glad you ain't goin' to whup me, Paw. I won't be bad any more. Just let me stay here and work in the show."

It took awhile for it to sink into me. But I finally got it. Alec Sherman, my stepson, was a grown man physically— but he was still an uneducated fifteen-year-old-kid, mentally and emotionally. I didn't stop to try and figure it. I just let it go that he'd either grown up simple, or maybe he'd taken a knock on the noggin somewhere that had retarded him mentally.

I talked to him some more to make sure I was right and there was no doubt about it. This big, skinny gawk that looked like a man about thirty-five had a kid's brain-power. I let him get cleaned up and gave him some chow. And all the time I watched him. He looked more like his mother than ever. And as I looked at him, all that old time hate for her—through him—came back to me. I decided to experiment.

I gave him a smart crack on the ear and stiffened, waiting to see if he'd come back at me. He didn't. He cringed and said: "What'd you do that for, Paw? I didn't do anything."

I knew then. I told him: "Shut your dam' trap and get to bed." And that's what he did. He piled into one of the bunks and corked off to sleep like a babe.

You won't believe this, but it's the Lord's truth.

I bought him another horn, told him the other'd got broken and put him out to tootin' it for attention in front of the kootch act, just before show time. Only it ain't called a kootch show anymore Old Nate Sherman's show's got class. We call it the *Artists and Models* show, now. Undraped Venuses, we call 'em. Rather, the barker does. We got a new spieler now, too. I don't break my tonsils anymore. This one's a dame. A nice gal, too. A sort of personal friend of mine, if you know what I mean. Her name is Diana Lynn.

This Diana is a smart cookie. It was she who first gives me the idea of changin' the name of the kootch show and dressing it up real fancy by building frames inside the tent and having the girls stand in artistic poses. For that I gave her ten percent interest in this particular show and we've both made money at it.

Diana used to be one of the girls in the show when it was still old-fashioned snake-hips and hula stuff. She wasn't so young, anymore. She was getting some lines in her little doll-like face and her blonde hair showed signs of too much bleach. But she kept her figure through dieting and rigorous exercise so that she could still put a lot of these young floozies to shame. Make believe she didn't know it, too, the tight dresses she always—

All right, I'm getting back to Alec. Diana is in this, too.

ANYHOW, with Alec and me, things just went back twenty years. I made him shine my shoes and run errands and when I'd get drunk and feeling mean, I strap him good. It was just like always. Except now that Alec was a grown man and it used to make me feel funny, treatin' him like that—but it made the revenge on his mother, Leah, that much more solid for me.

Oh, yeah, it was funny the way Alec was now, with that Artists and Models show where I made him work. On good chow he began to fill out a little; and cleaned up and all, he wasn't a bad-looking Joe. I guess some of the girls made a play for him, but he'd only get sore and embarrassed, like he used to when he was still a kid, physically. And when they'd get a little careless about paradin' around in their scanties, Alec would blush and twist his feet and get flustered as a boy as his first burlicue. In the contrary way of women, I reckon that made him more attractive to 'em. Some of them knocked themselves out tryin' to get a date. But he wouldn't have any part of any of 'em.

All this time, this Diana dame kept after me that it wasn't right to do Alec like I was doin'. She said I ought to take him to a doc and maybe try to help him. She was always fussin' around him like a mother hen around a chick. And that was funny, because he was as old as she was —in years.

I didn't think too much about Diana's

interest in Alec, at first. I thought she was just sorry for the big goon and tryin' to be nice to him. Several times she and I almost had rows about it when I tried to make her mind her own business and stay away from him.

As the weeks went by, too, I started to notice gradual, slight changes in Alec. He began to talk a little less like a kid and more like an adult. So slight a difference that you'd hardly notice it—just odd phrases, at times. And every once in awhile I'd catch him looking at me strangely and he'd get a little stubborn looking and just a mite less scared looking, when I'd have to smack him around for fallin' behind in his chores and stuff.

One day, I found out why that was. I came back to the Carny from some important business in the town we were playin' that week and I found Alec and this blonde Diana dame together in the *Artists And Models* show tent. It was about an hour before show time. Alec was reciting something from memory, and Diana was holding a book, watching and listening to him and checking him. They were so both absorbed they didn't hear me come into the tent at first.

I took one look at the expression on Diana's pretty, but kind of dissipated face, the way she was giving Alec the Double-O and I suddenly knew it was something more than being sorry for him, and kindness, that she felt for the guy. I'd seen that look on dames' faces before.

I said, sharp: "What the hell's goin' on, here?" I could feel temper rising like a flood inside of me, pounding in my ears and hurting my eyes. "What are them books? What are you two doin'?"

Alec jumped up as though a firecracker had been set off under him. He gaped at me, his mouth open, a scared look in his eyes, for a moment. He tried to say something and his mouth worked but no words came out.

Diana got up, too. She looked as nice as I'd ever seen her. Her blonde hair was newly bleached and set. She was wearing a simple little red-checked gingham dress, with puffed sleeves and a deeply squared neck. That beautiful figure of hers looked like it had been poured into the frock. She'd drive a guy crazy just to look at her.

She held her chin up proudly and said to me: "I've been teachin' Alec some school work. He has a right to learn it. We—well, we were goin' to tell you about it and surprise you, later. We've been workin' together for several weeks, now. We—"

"You have, now?" I said, stopping her cold. I walked toward them, slowly, measuredly. I got right up close to them. I said through my teeth: "Diana, get the hell out of here. If I catch you within ten yards of this monkey again, I'll thumb those blue, little, two-timin' eyes right out through the back of your head."

Then I turned to Alec. I said: "Go get my razor strop, you ugly dam' moron!"

HE SEEMED not to hear and just stood there, staring back at me, his eyes rolling, scared, a vein standing out alongside his forehead. I said: "Do as I say!" I gave him a full backhand blow across the mouth. Blood began to trickle slowly, crookedly, from one corner of his mouth. He began to shake. Then he found his voice:

He said: "You—you got to stop doin' that to me. Stop beatin' me. I ain't a kid anymore. Diana said so. She said I'm a man and you ain't got no right to treat me like you been doin'. She said I'm sick. I—"

I wheeled on Diana. I said: "Is that the kind of stuff you been fillin' his head full of? Why, you dumb, busybody blonde frill!"

She said: "Nate!" in a half scream, before my fist drove into her face. She went down. I turned back to Alec and his face was scarlet. He had his legs spraddled apart now, and his fists were balled at his sides. He said, softly, his voice breaking: "You can't do that to her!"

Then he swung and caught me a solid blow in the cheekbone that rattled my brain. I shook my head clear and saw him coming at me. I was caught short. My slinking, broken-spirited young puppy had finally become a full-grown fighting male animal, with his fangs bared. I had to fight. He swung again and I rolled with the punch and it slid off the top of my shoulder. I hit him once, in the mouth, again, but this time with my fist. He went back across the camp stools he and Diana had been sitting on. He came weaving up, spitting out blood and pieces of teeth. I missed the next swing and he caught me flush on the nose. I felt the bones go like an eggshell, crushed under somebody's boot.

We stood there for a minute, slugging, toe to toe, neither giving ground. I had him in weight and experience. I'd fought in "Hey, Rube!" carny battles in every hicktown on the circuit for over thirty years. But he had me in age and height and reach.

It was me who finally gave way and fell back, battered and bleeding. But he didn't give me a second's rest. He caught me in a flying tackle and I crashed back against a tent stake. We thrashed around on the ground, Alec battering me with his fists, in close, ruining my ribs and my gut. But from the corner of one eye, I saw a roustabout's knife that had been left sticking into a wooden stake.

With a desperate effort, I rolled free of Alec and got to my feet. I staggered toward that kinfe and picked it up. But he was right after me. I lunged at him with the blade, but he ducked under the blow and my arm swung down over his shoulder and rent a great slit in the back of the tent. Screams came ripping out

through that rent in the canvas. The girls who posed for this Artist and Models show, had their dressing tent back there.

At the same time Alec ducked under my knife thrust, he grabbed me around the knees and in a wild, fighting fury, lifted me clear off the ground and hurled me through that slit in the canvas right into the girl's dressing quarters.

I landed on a makeshift dressing table and smashed it to the floor, knocked over the girl who had been sitting before it. I remember her flying over on her back, a cute little redhead with long, graceful white legs kicking from the bottoms of her tights. I remember seeing the other girls, three of them, screaming, clutching towels and odd pieces of costume up in front of them, covering themselves, as they watched Alec come leaping on top of me.

The knife was gone from my hand, now and I didn't have much fight left. Alec lifted me up by the front of my tattered shirt and began hitting me with one fist, while he held me up with the other. He was a different man, now. The fierce fury of the fight had changed him even more. He had lost that little-boy look of fright and indecision. I'd never even seen a look on a guy's face like that, before.

He was beast-mean looking. It was as though he was takin' out all the trouble he'd ever had on me, and was makin' up for all the beatings I'd ever given him. I couldn't take much of that. He knocked me cold and kickin'.

Later, one of the girls said that after I dropped, Alec stood, shakin' himself all over. He looked different, they said. He didn't seem at all bothered, now, that half of them were only partly dressed. He looked all around at them, his lip curling a little. One of them started to bawl him out for wrecking the dressing room and he snarled at her to shut her painted face. Then he walked out. Nobody ever saw him again. Nor Diana Lynn, either. She must have gone with him. . .

Is there anything else you want to know, Miss, or do you think you got your fifty bucks worth? You still think Alec is the same guy as this Max Mercer, the trumpet man? . . . .

PART FOUR

MY NAME is Helen Walters and I work for a magazine called *Music World*. I do a personal chatter column for the *World*. Some interest had been stirred up about a couple of old records of Max Mercer's that had been recently unearthed. A music publisher was going to push some old songs of Mercer's. Max Mercer was going to be a big thing in the music world in a few months. So the magazine sent me out to find him and get a couple of columns on him. He'd sort of dropped out of the big cities and big bands for several years. Nobody was sure just where he could be found.

I found him, of course, at the Jackpot, a little southern, jump-dive roadhouse. Only I didn't really find him, then. I got there the last night he played and he had just left. I was driving back from there, into the nearest town, to put up at a hotel, along a road that ran along the bottom of a high cliff. My headlights caught for one flashing, horrible moment the picture of what looked like a body, hurtling down from the cliffs onto the big, jagged rocks, below. At the same time, above the roar of the car motor, I thought I heard a scream. I stopped and went back to investigate. I found a girl, lying smashed and broken and dying, on the rocks at the bottom of the cliff. She was still able to talk. Her name was Jennie Lee and you read her account of what happened that night.

It was patently true, except that she changed the last part of it, to make me think her suicide was murder by Max Mercer, so she could drag him to hell too.

She died before I left and since there was nothing I could do for her, I left her there, phoned the police anonymously where to find her. I didn't say anything about the story she'd told me.

I remembered what she'd said about the woman, Ina Courtney, and found out where Ina lived and went right there, hoping that Jennie Lee had guessed right and maybe I could find Max there. I reached the Courtney estate but before I rang the old-fashioned pull bell, I happened to glance through a narrow strip of window alongside the door.

I saw a woman in there bend over a fat old man on the floor and strike him over the head with a black object. I have never seen such an incredibly evil look on anyone else's face.

Then I saw another figure sprawled out on the floor, his face turned toward the door. From pictures I'd seen, I recognized Max Mercer. The rest you already know, from the account of Ina Courtney, herself, which you have read.

I got that story from her, under threat of testifying that I saw her kill her husband. Later, from the papers, I found out that she told the police the original story that she had planned, that her husband had fallen downstairs. She didn't mention Max Mercer, at all. She knew better.

If she had, I would have gone right to the police with my story. Some day soon, when Max—or Alec—is completely himself again, he and I, together, will go back down there and face that thing out. We can't let that woman get away with cold-blooded murder. I think the extenuating circumstances will cover our delay in getting to this.

That night, at the Courtney place, when Max ran out of the house, I called to him and tried to stop him, but he was too full of panic. He got away from me.

From the things that Ina Courtney had told me—the strange effect of that blow on the head—part of which I saw and heard, myself, while standing outside the front door, I knew that a terrible thing had happened to Max Mercer.

Later, I told the whole thing to a psychiatrist friend of mine. We talked it over at great length. From all these accounts which I let him read, he decided that when Alec Sherman had been a boy of approximately fifteen, he'd been hit by an automobile and suffered a severe head injury, which resulted in total amnesia.

The second blow on the head, twenty years later, received from Ina Courtney, wiped out the intervening stage and sent Alec plunging back to the time of the first accident so that he now remembered nothing whatsoever of the personality, Max Mercer, that he had taken during that time.

The statement I later got from Nate Sherman, Alec's stepfather, the carnival man, proved all that to be true. It took me some time to find Nate Sherman and again, of course, I was too late. It was another six months before I caught up with Max Mercer again.

I traced him, this time, through a piano man I knew who had played with Max several times. He'd seen Max, he swore, in a big midwestern city. He'd been with a blonde young woman. I hunted him down in the neighborhood where he'd been seen and finally found the name, *Diana Lynn,* in the doorbell tab of a small walkup flat in a rundown section of the city. I went inside and climbed three flights of the dirty tile steps with the kids' chalk scrawling on the cracked plaster. I came to the door of apartment 3C and stopped. I caught my hand halfway up to knock and held it.

I STOOD there, goosebumps working out over me, and listened. From inside came the wail of trumpet music. That horn was taking off on a "preachin' blues" number that tore at your heart

and curled your insides and split your nerves and strummed at them. It was music that held all the inner, forlorn and wailing sadness of the deep south's kinky-headed levee workers, where it originated —and all their love and laughter, too.

I recognized that tone, those knocked-out riffs. There was only one man in the world could do those things on a horn. It was Max Mercer in there and he'd come all the way back. He was playing like he always used to. Now that I knew my long search was over, I got weak in the knees. I took a deep breath and rapped on the door, long and hard.

The music cut off. Footsteps came toward the door and it was thrust open. A woman stood there, with her head cocked, eyeing me. She was better than average height and she fitted Nate Sherman's description, except that it hadn't done her figure justice. She was wearing a cotton wrapper and apparently little else. When one woman says another is really built, you can bet that she's all the cover and pin-up girls rolled into one. I say Diana Lynn was really put together.

But she wasn't very pretty right now. There were dark rings under her eyes and tiny crows feet at their corners. Her complexion, without makeup, was grainy. It was obvious that she'd taken more than a few drinks and that didn't help any.

I said: "I'm sorry to disturb you, but I—I'd like to see Max Mercer . . . or perhaps I should say, Alec Sherman."

She started a little and her eyes went over me, taking in my trim, tailored suit, my glasses—and it was as though I could see into her brain, where she was thinking: *You, too, honey? You don't look the type. I wouldn't think Maxie would go for the pert and prissy intellectual type.*

She should have known better. When it comes to a man like Max Mercer, outward appearance doesn't count—it's the things inside a woman, long hidden, long surpressed, but always there.

A little surly, she said: "He ain't here."

I raised my brows. "Please. It—it's very important. I heard him playing in there, while I was knocking. *Please* let me see him!"

She said: "Who the hell are you, anyhow? What do you want with him?"

I told her who I was and blurted out most of my story, saying that I wanted to tell it to Max, himself, that I thought he ought to know. What I didn't tell her, though, was the way I felt about Max, personally, and that now I was as bad as Jennie Lee or Ina Courtney—or even Diana Lynn, herself.

"Come inside," she said.

I stepped past her, along a short hall and into a small, dingy, one-room flat. She stood behind me. She said: "All right, you didn't believe me. Well, look around. See for yourself. He's not here."

I saw that she was telling the truth. I started to ask her about the music I had heard and then I saw the radio-phonograph in the corner. There was a stack of records on the table beside it. I went over and looked at them and they were all Max Mercer recordings.

"I see," I said. "Do you expect him back?"

SHE WINCED and for a moment she had to control a puckering chin. She finally shook her head. "No. I don't think so," she said in a faraway voice. "I don't count on him comin' back." Her face semed to break all up and she walked to a table and picked up a shot glass full of whiskey and downed it.

"I'll tell you," she said then. "Max was here—but he's gone. He was comin' along fast and was just about back to normal again. Then one day, he started playing some old recordings of mine. He hit one, with a trumpet solo feature by Max Mercer. He listened and then he played it again, looking sick and pale and with his thin face all tight and sort of

a crazy light in his eyes. He played that record several times, then fished through the rest of them and pulled out some more Max Mercer stuff. He played them for three hours."

She took another drink and went on: "Then he shut the thing off and turned to me. He said: 'Diana, you know who that was, playin' that horn? That was me, Diana.' I thought he'd gone off his rocker for sure, then. He didn't say anymore. He jumped up and ran out."

"That was the last you saw of him?"

She shook her head. "He came back. He brought a trumpet back with him. I don't know where he got it. I never found out. Without a word, then, he sat down and started playing. It gave me the creeps, because it *was* the same as those records he'd played. You couldn't make any mistake. When he was through, he said: 'Diana, I'm Max Mercer.' . . . I just looked at him and said: 'I guess you are, Alec, I guess you are.'"

"What happened then?"

She shrugged and poured herself another slug of cheap whiskey. "Nothing much," she said. "He went out that night and didn't come back until late. Then he told me he had a job, playin' trumpet in a swing dive down on Kelly Street. He was different from then on. I—well, I just couldn't seem to get through to him. We suddenly weren't talkin' the same language. One night he went out and he didn't come back. I went down to this place he was playin' and he was gone from there, too. So was a little black-haired scat singer who'd been with the band. Nobody knew where."

I had held onto my purse so hard, my knuckles stood out whitely, all the time she was talking. I waited awhile and when she didn't say anymore, I told her: "Thank you, Miss Lynn." I felt a little dazed and sort of sick inside. "I—I'll be going now." I started for the door.

(Please continue on page 97)

Robot's Betrayal

He watched her —and was filled with a hollow ache.

Justin won the deadly rat race over a billing machine—and Margie . . . when he kissed his guts good-by.

◆ ◆ ◆

By Henry Guth

IF you beat a billing machine long enough, you go crazy. There is something about the damn thing that gets you.

Justin pounded the machine with his fingers. In his mind he was beating the life out of it. Smashing it to bits, because he was a slave to it—and because it had made him kill a man.

"Inconceivable . . . inconceivable . . . incon . . ." he wrote.

He ripped the bills off the machine, tore them into fine pieces and dropped them in the basket. He put a dummy bill on the pile and marked it void and gave it a number the same as the one he'd ruined.

He sat and looked at the machine. The damn machine. Hating it, wanting to beat it to pieces for what it had done to him.

When Ben came in and Margie, the bookkeeper, he calmed down. He listened to Ben working the comptometer and Margie working the bookkeeping machine in the center of the room. They both made lightening-fast mechanical sounds.

For the first time he saw all this in perspective. The way it must look to an outsider. What he saw was Margie and Ben and himself being slaves to machines. Almost being machines themselves.

It surprised him to find this out. He remembered when he thought running a fan biller was fine, useful work—when it wouldn't have occurred to him that it could drive him to kill anybody.

* * *

He knew Ben briefly from way back. Two years ago. A long time. Since then he'd stumbled around the country and come back to Los Angeles with a hollow loneliness inside him. And nowhere was there anyone to fill the loneliness. He began hating the world, thinking of it as a pressure on him, and thinking of the hardness needed to resist it.

Ben was a human dynamo. A short wiry man with a Roman nose. He talked and thought and worked like a riveter. He was the fastest typist Justin had ever seen. A fan-fold biller made blurring sounds when Ben worked it.

With a wife and four kids, Ben had to worry about raising them; especially the girl who was fourteen. He assessed tariffs at Local Cartage eight hours each day, and billed at Northern Freight four hours each night. He needed money to raise his kids.

He was a funny guy, a philanthropist without money. He got satisfaction out of helping people. People like Justin who were disillusioned about the world. He said all Justin needed was a girl.

Ben got him the job at Local Cartage. The boss didn't want another biller but Ben talked him into it. The boss was a big man and angry that he couldn't use

Justin. He went around swearing there wasn't enough work for four people to do and he had to pay such lousy wages. The boss was all right.

Justin was afraid of the job at first. He couldn't believe his luck. All these friends around. And thirty dollars a week wasn't bad. Maybe the sunlight was breaking through. Maybe he could live now, like a human being.

The first time he worked the fan biller he was nervous. He made mistakes and ruined a lot of bills. This scared him. He wanted to make good. Wanted to hold onto this job.

The billing machine was an ordinary typewriter with attachments. A continuous roll of paper, nine sheets thick, came up from a box on the floor behind. Eight long carbons on jack-knife blades between the sheets. You typed up a bill. Then you yanked up the sheets, slapped back the carbons and ripped off nine copies. Ben could do it in half a second.

With the billing machine you didn't have to be delicate. The harder you slammed the thing the better it worked. You pounded a tabulator with the palm of your right hand, pounded hard, two dozen times a minute, and the carriage with its heavy fan-fold rig crashed against its stop. The machine was rugged.

Justin whaled the daylights out of the machine, working off the bitterness in him, and the machine took it. He had to marvel. He had to respect the machine.

On his left was Cliff Franchise, working the other billing machine. Cliff was slow but experienced. He waded through split tariffs and split consignments without hesitation. He had fuzz on his chin. He always wore a clean white shirt. He smiled often and liked giving Justin a hand. He didn't look as though he'd ever been lonely.

On Justin's right were Ben and the comptometer. Ben played the comptometer like a pianist with his left hand, a cigarette hanging from his lips, and scrawled freight rates and charges on bills of lading with his right. He did this hour after hour, talking a blue streak and cocking his head and squinting against the smoke of his cigarette. Whenever work slowed, he got up and found something else to do. He couldn't sit still.

Margie worked quietly at a desk behind. She used a pen mostly, making entries in books. Once in awhile she typed up statements or worked the bookkeeping machine, sitting on the high stool in the center of the room. She had a smooth white complexion, black hair and startlingly beautiful legs. She rode the bus in every day from Hollywood. She seemed never to have opinions about anything.

Justin got used to these people and got over being lonely. He thought they were good people and he learned to smile again and kid around. He even grew attached to the billing machine.

But Ben wasn't satisfied. "Why don't you and Margie get together?" he said.

Justin jumped. The iron wall descended —the rigid iron wall he'd fought all his life. Girls were soft and mysterious. He wanted them, craved them, but was afraid of them. It was terrible to want something that way.

He felt like a orphan in a new home for about three weeks. And then it was Christmas.

The boss gave everybody a ball-point pen. They took up a collection and bought him a set of luggage.

The boss was angry. He roared around all day, bawling out truck drivers for nothing and finding billing mistakes that didn't exist.

That night he was furious. "I have to lay off somebody!" he said. He looked at the floor and roared. "Can't keep two billers on the job!" He hated himself and was furious. But the holiday rush was over and he could do nothing about it. He went on:

"Somebody has to go." He glared at Justin. "You and Cliff decide which it will be. I'll keep you both on another week, and then raise the one left to thirty-five a week!"

He left it up to them, to decide between them.

Justin went home to his room and lay on the bed. He was cold and he felt the emptiness echoing around the room. Time stretched back and was full of bleakness. He couldn't see ahead at all. There it was all blank and forbidding.

He couldn't sleep.

CLIFF was the same for five days, but he was changed. He still smiled and was friendly and helpful. But he seemed smug. He didn't seem upset about the job. A job was only a job. And maybe he thought he had seniority and it was assured him.

But he said, "It doesn't matter to me. I'll look around for another."

Ben thought he might work out something with Northern Freight where he worked nights.

But he couldn't. Northern was a big company and had a complete office force. It was impersonal about employees. So much work, so many machines, so many men. Cut and dried. The holiday rush was over.

Ben suggested to Justin: "You need some relaxation. Go to a movie with Margie."

The thought welling up in him almost drove Justin crazy. How could he take Margie to the movies? A soft, lithe girl like that? He watched her sinuous movements—and was filled with a hollow ache. She was so damn beautiful.

Justin began hating the machine, and was filled with desire for it at the same time. He pounded it like an enemy, then quieted down, alarmed that he might break it and lose the job. He was careful and angry by fits and starts.

Ben worked his comptometer with no more worries than usual. He was preoccupied with his wife and kids. The comptometer continued to sing under his hand.

Margie kept to herself. She talked seldom and with impartial soberness.

Justin prowled the city at night alone, to feel again how it was. It was bad.

He found out where Cliff lived—in a boarding house on Seventh. The street was dark and there and an alley ran between the house and the saloon next door. That's what he found out.

He despised the machine—for what it was doing to him, and for the passionate attachment he had to it. He beat hell out of it, but it did no good.

Margie Tanner, it kept saying through the crash of metal. Margie Tanner . . . Margie Tanner . . . Margie . . . Margie . . . Margie . . .

Freight bills fused into the image of Margie by the magic of the machine. They fused into home and kids and vague feelings of happiness. Insecure happiness. Menaced happiness.

Sometimes it all disappeared and only pavements were left. Through the pounding and ripping of the machine he walked the pavements and felt again the awful loneliness.

Cliff didn't find another job.

His girl came over one night. A cripple. One leg in iron braces, which clumped when she walked. She was pretty though, and vivacious. She filled the office with innocent gayety. She seemed unaware of anything in the world except love. She jabbered happily about the bicycle Cliff had bought her so she could strengthen her leg.

Justin hated the girl. He hated her and loved her at the same time. She was innocent and pure and he hated her because she made him afraid. He caressed the keys of his machine with a fierce possessiveness.

Everybody had a girl. Cliff had one. He didn't need the job. He didn't need Margie. He didn't need anything. He could work somewhere else.

The boss became a tyrant, unreasonable and cruel. The machine made mistakes. Sometimes the bills Justin was copying blurred and he had to guess at the figures. He always guessed wrong.

The boss seemed glad to find something legitimate to rage about. "Dammit!" he roared. "You've been here over three weeks! Why the hell can't you learn split tariffs!" He roared like a bull, and went out and roared at the drivers.

The atmosphere was ugly.

"Take Margie out," Ben persisted. "You're tightened up. Getting jittery. You'll bust if you don't have some fun."

Justin swore. She'd given no sign. She couldn't like him. He'd probably bore her. But he had to hold the job; had to or he would have no chance at all with her.

Margie retired even more. She buried herself in her books. She was a shadow in the room—only her lovely legs seared an image in his thoughts.

Ben's hair-trigger mind thought up a thousand job solutions an hour. He rattled them off as he worked, squinting against the cigarette smoke. Try this, try that, and this and that and that.

But they were all no good. Justin didn't want another job. He wanted this one. The people, the machine and the girl.

He stood it for five days. Margie's lush image bored into his dreams, and he clung to the machine with fear-stricken tenacity. His tongue became parched from smoking interminable cigarettes.

After work on the fifth day he hid himself in the alley between the saloon and the boarding house. Cliff came down about ten o'clock and went into the saloon for a beer. His girl came to the saloon and they both went away.

Justin hid in the alley and hated them and hated himself.

Cliff came back, walking alone, after midnight. As he walked past the alley, Justin hit him with a brick, visciously.

Then he hurled the brick through the window of the saloon. It made a terrific racket and as he ran he heard voices crying out in anger and excitement.

HE faced the machine and loathed it with his eyes. It had an ugly personality he hadn't noticed before. It was smug and leering about something.

He banged it with his fist. But it wouldn't break. It was a rugged machine.

Ben was in a curious state of inactivity. He sat at his desk looking at the comptometer, not even smoking. It was uncanny to see Ben quiet.

Margie rustled paper with a dry rattling sound and seemed to fumble a lot.

The boss came in and he was mild and pale. He was almost unrecognizable without an apoplectic red face. The anger seemed surprised out of him.

He talked in wondering tones about the riot at the saloon. "Somebody threw a brick through the window," he said.

"Some drunk threw a brick through the window. A fight started and Cliff was killed." He leaned heavily against the bookkeeping machine and looked around the office as though it were someplace he'd never been before. "He was a good kid—"

Then his anger flared up again. He turned, enraged, to Justin. "So you'll stay on at thirty-five a week!"

Ben looked over with strangely mild eyes, sad eyes. "Okay kid. It's a hell of a way for it to happen, but maybe it's fate." He snapped like a rubber band then, and stretched a nervous hand to his comptometer. He played it like a jazz pianist.

Margie smiled reassuringly, as though she were glad he was staying despite how it had happened. A special smile.

It broke something inside Justin.

He ran his hands over the billing machine, feeling the cold metal, suddenly aching all over for something soft. Something alive and warm, to temper the hardness of the machine—the hardness he felt in himself. It made him desperate.

Why hadn't she smiled *that way* sooner? Why the hell hadn't she?

He tapped the keys, and they responded obediently. He slapped the tab, and it responded. Everything responded obediently to his touch.

He saw the machine as a symbol.

His head seemed to swell with horror. He wondered, marveled how he had become a slave to this insensible object.

Ben handed over a pile of bills, and yelped when Justin knocked them out of his hand. The cigarette fell out of Ben's mouth.

Justin pulled the machine from the bench. He dropped it to the floor. It crashed, rent, and broke.

He left the office, left everything. He had only a wild desire to lock himself up, away from the world.

He looked for a policeman.

A Crimson Shroud

She pressed back against the rear counter. . . .

By Bruce Cassiday

I TURNED slowly from my coffee and studied the guy who had just come into Betty's midnight coffee joint. He was wearing a gray hat and a gray coat. His hat was pulled down over his gray face, and the brims were turned down. He was spending a lot of energy watching no one, and his gray eyes were directly ahead of him.

I'd seen him Thursday night at the gas station outside Santa Barbara, staring up at a whiskey sign. I'd seen him Wednesday noon in San Miguel at a bar, talking to a salesman in a checker suit. I'd seen him getting off the hot bus in San José,

57

looking sweaty and drawn. There was no mistaking him—he'd made himself so self-effacing he stood out like a sore hind leg.

Betty Hiller came out from the grill and said: "Hello, King. Glad to see you back in town. Rupert was wanting—" Then she saw the gray man and she stopped. She looked at me a second, read my eyes, and turned to him.

"What'll it be, mister?"

The gray man's voice was so low I could hardly hear it. It was soft and it had a lisp to it. "A Danish and a coffee, miss."

Betty got the coffee and Danish and set them on the counter. She came over and looked at me. Her eyes were question marks. I poured down a mouthful of her coffee and said:

"Anything new?"

She shook her head. "Any cute nurses in the hospital, King?"

"The beauty of hospital crones is a highly over-rated commodity, kid."

"I hope so. . . . Did this one go good, King?" She couldn't bring herself to mention it. Some people are funny.

"The transfusion? Yeah. It was all right. I'm getting used to them. Hell, that's what makes life interesting."

She pulled out a rag from under the counter and made a couple swipes at the linoleum top. "Uh huh. You—you look better."

"Like hell," I grinned. I took a squint in the twisted mirror in back of her. My face was about three shades whiter than a corpse's. There were black pouches under my eyes. The big blue vein in my forehead was plain even in that beat-up chipped glass.

The gray man dropped a quarter on the counter and got up. He went out through the door without looking at either of us.

"He'll be waiting at the corner for me," I told Betty.

"Are you sure he's one of them?"

"I saw him in San José, San Miguel, Santa Barbara, and now tonight. He's so bad he's good. New technique. He shows up so bright I'm supposed to think he's a coincidence."

"King, give it all up. You come out here and let me take care of you. You're not meant for this kind of life."

"What? This perfect set-up? Miss all these big pay checks of Prince Rupert's because it's dangerous?"

Her eyes were tired then—tired and hopeless. "All right, King."

"Besides, I kind of enjoy it." That was twisting the knife.

She went on wiping the counter over the mess the gray man had left. "King, I have cash saved up. I have a place here, and I could take care of you."

"But look at all the easy dough I'd be missing! I'm the perfect alibi, kid! No one'd ever suspect *me* of—of that type of work."

"But you're never careful! You always manage to get some kind of a nick in the finger, or on the hand."

I could see her fingers were tightly dug into the cloth on the counter and that she was bearing down on it with all her weight.

"And what?"

"Nothing."

"And I'll probably kill myself one of these days."

She turned to me. "And you'll probably die one of these days because you're such a damned fool. Oh, you big damned fool!"

"Look, Betty," I said. "It's a perfect set-up. It can't be beat. Sure, it's a gamble, but what isn't? There isn't anyone who'd suspect me. An invalid—pulling down a gunman's salary? Nonsense!"

"But King!"

"Anyway, I've got the best doctor in Los Angeles in case I ever do get another cut. Dr. Harold Horner. He knows more about transfusions and blood than anyone else in the business. Anytime I get the slightest cut, I ring him up. And he's on Prince Rupert's payroll. He's okay."

"I know, King, but—"

"But, but, but! But what? I've picked up ten thousand dollars in the past year."

"And you said then you'd quit and—"

"I can make more! And then, later, maybe—"

"I'm afraid now! The police must have found out."

"No. This guy's one of Blackie Hansen's men, honey. He picked me up in San José right after I'd gotten out of the hospital. Hansen's located in San José. I thought I'd managed to duck him."

"But he'll try to kill you."

"No, baby. He's just down here to find out where Prince Rupert's set-up is. Then he'll wire back."

"And then?"

"There'll be no 'and then,' baby. I'll get him tonight, before he finds anything out. Funny as hell he's so damned uncagy about it. Trying to make me think he's an accident."

I grinned, studying my face in the mirror. "I sure do look like hell, don't I?"

Betty's eyes got that womanly way again, as if all her heart and stomach and soul were in them. "You look weak, King. Oh, Lord, you look weak and like you needed me."

"What would be the good of us, baby? There'd always be me in the way of anything we wanted to do. There'd always be the possibility I'd cut myself and bleed to death in a minute. If you ever got to be dependent on me, you'd be the one to go through all the hell."

"But King—"

"No, Betty. It's no good. The blood of kings, that's what it is. The blood of dead kings. I wouldn't want to curse anybody else with it—ever."

She pressed back against the rear counter hard, slowly shaking her head.

I stood up, dropped a quarter on the linoleum. "I'll be all right. You just worry about that man in gray." I had my rod out then, checking the clip, jamming a last shell in.

"Oh, King! Please don't. You don't have to, do you?"

"Maybe I enjoy it, Betty. Maybe I like to kill people—because they're happy, and they can have things I can never have . . . Maybe that's it."

And I walked out into the dark.

It was a perfect set-up, working for Prince Rupert in that Los Angeles ring. Hell, here I was the sickest-looking thing alive on the streets. Who'd ever suspect me of risking death to bump off a guy now and then for the Prince? Until now, nobody'd even thought of bothering me.

No one except Betty. And she'd always bothered me—a different kind of bother. What's a guy like me got to offer a girl? Nothing but my damned hemophilia. . . .

The rod was in my pocket, feeling cool and good to the fingers. I walked down the sidewalk to the first dark alleyway south of Betty's night shop. I'd better dispose of this clinker before I led him home and tipped him off to Prince Rupert's hide-out.

He was in the end of the alleyway, waiting. I couldn't see him at all, but I knew he was there. Something about my instincts. Maybe guys like me who're walking hand in hand with death all the time sort of develop a second sight.

I turned down the alley, walking slowly, my heels making choppy sounds on the cement. The echoes cut back from the end —it was a dead end. I walked forward, my hands out carefully, trying to feel in front of me.

Just as I was about two yards from the end of the alleyway—I could tell I was that close by the way the night closed in on me, and the way the echoes set up a closer clatter—I heard a shifting in the dark. There was a half-silly grunt, and a shuffling of feet.

I pulled the rod out then, and I knew right where to shoot. I stood still, drawing a line down the dark, evening it up on the heart. It's always easier there, quicker. The other shots down in the belly are messy as hell, and take too damned long. A guy can tell a life history in the time between the first drop of blood and the last twitch.

"Wait!" the guy grated out in a tight little voice. The voice still had that insidious little lisp, and the tone was soft and gentle. A killer if there ever was one. We're a breed unto ourselves.

I laughed softly. It sounded like the laugh a corpse might grate out inside his coffin. The night around us was a lot like the dark of a coffin, at that. I laughed again.

"Good-by, killer," I said.

Then I blasted out a shot quickly. The blast of the sound bounced around inside the blind alley for a few moments and then died out.

"Wait, King! Don't kill me! You can't shoot me!"

"I just want you to take something back to Blackie Hansen, pal. Tell him I'm acknowledging receipt of his invitation to death—with lead!"

I pumped three more shots into him, and I heard a lot of gasping and heavy sighing. And then a garbage lid clanged drunkenly on the cement, and I could hear a body slide down a wall onto the ground. A piece of heavy cloth ripped and tore. Then a head hit the cement hard.

I bent over the body and fumbled through the clothes. The damn fool was still breathing.

"King! You fool! *You damned fool!*" he said over and over again. And then suddenly, choking back the death rattle for a short instant, he let out a low little chuckle, and it was a laugh of death. It had the sound of gray gravestones to it.

"Little man, don't laugh so hard," I grinned. "It's you that's dying tonight, not me."

I pulled the junk out of his pockets and laid it on the cement. I wanted to make sure just who this guy was so I could tell Prince Rupert. Hell, Prince'd probably give me a five-hundred bonus for this job. The Prince's a pretty good guy if you treat him right.

I struck a match and scooped the junk up into my hands, as fast as I could. No good having a big crowd watching me shake down a warm corpse. I was so nervous from excitement and weakness my hands were shaking.

"Damn it!"

The fool had carried one of those stupid nail files in his pocket. And now I stared down at my hand, and at the slow crimson spot forming on my palm, growing and growing and growing as I watched it.

I doused the light. It was all a matter of time, now. Back to Betty's place. Call Doctor Horner. Bandage the hand up. Nothing to worry about. It meant another transfusion probably. Nothing to worry about—keep a cool head. . . .

Something in my eyes must have tipped Betty off the instant I pulled the door open. She ran around the counter and bent over my hand, pulling the handkerchief off fast, looking down.

"Oh, King!" she gasped, and closed the handkerchief around my hand, almost with a helpless little caress.

"Call Dr. Horner. If you can't get him, get Dr. Lewis. I've got a long list of doctors I can trust."

"I have to bandage this up, King. You'll lose too much blood by the time I can get a call through."

She led me behind the counter and tossed a bandage around my hand out of a first-aid kit. Then, while I sat down in a chair, she went over to the telephone.

I suddenly thought of the junk in my pocket. I took it all out, glanced at an address book belonging to Dick Harrison, and went into the kitchen. There was an incinerator outside and I dumped all the stuff into it and lit it.

I got back inside just as Betty completed the connection.

"Dr. Horner?"

I could hear Horner's voice blaring out loudly through the receiver. He always talked as if there were a hurricane.

"Yeah?"

"Dr. Horner. This is Betty Hiller. It's King Lansing again. He's cut his hand. It's nothing bad, but we want you to fix it up right away."

"Uh huh. Can you come in here to me?"

"Sure. I've got my car."

"Bring along Harrison, too."

"Harrison?"

"Sure. He's with King."

"With King?"

"King's last transfusion in San José brought on a couple of complications. An odd reaction in his blood. Prince Rupert hired Dick Harrison to stick to King in case anything happened. Harrison's the only one available in miles with the correct RH factor. We didn't want to tell King for fear of scaring him too much."

I heard it all. The crimson was seeping through out under the handkerchief now, running off onto my clothes, and dropping in a tight little ever-widening pool on the floor.

The blood of kings—the blood of very dead kings.

And Betty got it too, the same time I did. Her face was drained of color when she hung up. She sat there and stared at me and watched me get weaker and weaker.

Adventures into

The GHOSTS of MONT ST. MICHEL

No building the age of the abbey of Mont St. Michel, with its dank dungeons and gloomy chambers, is without its quota of ghosts. Of the spooks who walk those ancient halls, we do not know. The ghosts we speak of here are not imaginary, but real, and can be seen today by anyone who will travel to France.

These specters do not haunt the abbey itself, but haunt the sands that surround the mount when the tide recedes, leaving a desolation that stretches farther than the eye can see.

In the fall, winter and spring, fishermen risk their lives along these barren reaches. Three dangers threaten -- tide, quicksand and fog. The tide roars across the more than seven miles of sand faster than a horse can gallop and has doomed many a luckless stranger caught in its path. But the fishermen can calculate the rise of the tide. Quicksands, though treacherous, can be crossed by those who know how. The one thing these fishermen most fear is fog.

the UNKNOWN

BY-
Frederick
Blakeslee
No 2

THE FOG SHUTS DOWN OVER THE DESERT OF SAND WITH INCREDIBLE SPEED, AND IS SOMETIMES SO THICK ONE CANNOT SEE HIS OWN KNEES OR OUTSTRETCHED HAND. ALONE, IN SUCH CASES, A FISHERMAN IS IN REAL DANGER, AND OFTEN MEETS DEATH BY TIDE, QUICKSAND OR BOTH. BUT IN PARTIES OF THREE OR MORE, THEY CAN SOMETIMES OUTWIT THE FOG, KEEPING THEIR DIRECTION BY CHANGING PLACES, THUS

WHEN THE FOG SHUTS DOWN THE "GHOSTS" BEGIN TO WALK. THEY APPEAR IN FEARSOME SHAPES WHICH MEN, LOST IN THE MURKY GLOOM, NEVER FAIL TO SEE. THE UNCANNY PART IS THAT OFTEN THE SHAPES ASSUME AN UNMISTAKABLE HUMAN FORM. THEY ARE EVEN RECOGNIZABLE, AND ALWAYS OF A MAN LONG DEAD!

FISHERMEN WILL SWEAR BY THIS RECOGNITION, EVEN AFTER THEY ARE SAFE AT THE MOUNT. THE SERIOUSNESS WITH WHICH THESE STORIES ARE ACCEPTED MAY BE GAUGED BY THE FACT THAT MASSES ARE SAID FOR THE REPOSE OF THE DEAD MAN'S SOUL.

WHAT ARE THESE FORMS? WHAT CAUSES THEM?

GRAVEYARD QUEEN

Susi remained standing, smiling. . . .

By H. Hassell Gross

Sleazy Susi Olah couldn't lose her rancorous war with men—because she played . . . for keeps.

THE windows of Susi Olah's one-room flat in Budapest stood open to the stifling summer air. Sprawled on a couch, eyes half-shut in sullen brooding, nineteen-year-old Susi heard laughter on the street below. It was some girl out for a Sunday walk and loitering with her sweetheart.

Susi's lip curled with hatred—hatred

of the men who avoided her or else laughed at her square face and fat, short legs. Fools! Couldn't they see that she had more brains than all the pretty pieces they loved and left? But that was what they couldn't stand—a woman with brains. The treacherous curs couldn't fool a smart girl, betray her. . . .

Susi's slitted eyes opened angrily and fell on the flies struggling on a strip of flypaper laid on the window sill. Their puny efforts to escape the sticky mess fascinated and amused her. How soon they died! If only men could be made to die as quickly!

A stray bit of knowledge, a fact or two learned during the nurse's training, slowly forced its way to the surface of Susi's mind. Flypaper—arsenic. She caught her breath and for a moment the heavy, brooding face was almost pretty. Then she rose, took a cup of water to the window and, carefully brushing away the dead flies, tore off a strip of the treated paper.

Below in the street, the pretty girls passed with their dates, red-shirted peasants and Army men on leave. Budapest was gayer than ever, it seemed to Susi who was suddenly no longer lonely—or powerless. The flypaper soaking there in the cracked cup would from now on be her elixir. Elixir of arsenic—Susi liked the phrase.

A few weeks later, she moved into the village of Nagyrev, sixty miles from Budapest. The isolated little settlement, without a railroad and lacking a doctor or even a priest, was carefully chosen for her plans. In Nagyrev, life was simple and brutal. Like many Hungarian farming communities, the village had more men than women.

Frequent wife-beatings and just as frequent exchange of wives, without consulting the woman, were common. The men solved their problems by muscle power; but a woman must use wit and cunning to get rid of a dull bacon-bringer and gain a younger, more ardent lover.

The contest between the sexes was unequal; but with Susi to band the women together and supply the nectar that could work wonders with strained domestic relations, things would be different. Susi giggled to herself. She'd never been married, but she certainly knew what to do about husbands!

She spread the news that she was a nurse, very experienced and much superior to the two old crones usually called to attend the village sick. To prove it, she showed the little bottles of medicine prepared by herself and for sale at one hundred pegoe each or, roughly, seventeen dollars. "They are not for everybody," she announced. "Only for those I think need them."

The first experiments had to be made carefully. She must establish herself first, learn which women were most dissatisfied, which ones could safely be approached with hints of a new way to play with men for keeps.

But patients—and clients—came fast enough. Overworked, mistreated women need a sympathetic ear; a close-mouthed nurse can have all their secrets in a single afternoon. And if there is a sick child, the last, puny, unwanted one of a dozen or so. . . .

Susi learned to watch the mother's eyes, to listen for the murmur: "It's a pity. So many—I haven't the time for this one." Sometimes it mounted to a scream: "Filthy, whining brat! Never a second to rest!"

The silent nurse would smile. *A sick infant is easy,* she would think. Presently, when it was safe, she would show her magic bottle. "To take care of your troubles." She knew when comprehension dawned in the woman's eyes. "To relieve you of—everything."

She was right. One sip from the spoon so tenderly held by the mother—Susi always made sure it was not *her* hand on the handle—and the ailing babe suffered no more.

From children to husbands is not a long step. Susi and the women of Nagyrev made it easily. Before the nurse's first year was up, at least two husbands had been stricken by a mysterious, new disease which only Susi could diagnose. But men are more dangerous than children. They grow suspicious so quickly, and then they make trouble.

Susi went to see her two competitors. She had a scheme, she said, for dividing the district among the three of them; would they come to her home for a secret conference? They came, trusting and liking Susi as all women did. Immediately thereafter the "sickness" carried them off.

She kept another step ahead of the game by doing what she had never been able to do before—she got herself a husband. He was a credulous old widower, the father of the handsome local *halotkem,* or police coroner.

Georges was a virtuous youth, but the pick of the village for strength. Susi could scarcely contain herself long enough to see that his old father passed on. She watched the old man breathe his last, then promptly made a pass at the son.

Love, Susi learned, is a little different from murder; a gal needs to be more subtle when not dealing with corpses. And if the man involved has just seen his father die in convulsive agony, it may be slightly unwise to snuggle up to him on the funeral night. It may even be smarter not to snuggle at all.

Susi had a time trying to convince righteous Georges that she wasn't a thoroughly bad woman. Finally, it got too much even for one of her iron nerve. She poured a little derivative of arsenic into the soup and went out to relax with the girls.

When Georges caught up with her, he was bent double with stomach pains, but he could still talk—and point a pistol. From inside the tavern where she was schooling a couple of misunderstood wives, Susi heard his raving threats. She left her seat and walked stolidly out to the street.

"Georges," she pronounced nonchalantly, "is evidently dying of the sickness."

Before them all, he raised his pistol and fired. At the same moment, he fell down in agony. Susi remained standing, smiling . . . unharmed.

ONLY magic could have prevented him from missing so wide a target, and the whole village was impressed. Now she was really the queen of Nagyrev. As for Georges, he was so filled with superstitious awe that she allowed him to recover. Befuddled, he puttered about her, assuring everybody that the sickness was dreadful, Susi was a saint.

As coroner, he now pronounced every death a natural one. He was honest. Susi had cured him, hadn't she? And if she couldn't cure others, they just—naturally—died.

The village graveyard now began to reap the harvest Susi had intended from the beginning. Almost every week, some unhappy woman put on her black shawl and went to visit the nurse. For years the men died with the suddenness of flies, sometimes at home, more often in the fields after eating from the lunch pail put up by their devoted wives, and once three of them publicly and together in the tavern where Susi was having a quiet beer.

Strangely, there was almost no distrust of her. At first she made the course of death run erratically. Just when the men began to mutter that only husbands and lovers suffered from the sickness, a group of ailing old people or a few sickly children would die.

Toward the end, however, she had begun to branch out toward the nearby village of Tiszakurt, Susi scarcely bothered to be cautious. Even the burgomeister, when he dared an upstart question about the speed with which her patients passed away, grew pale and stammered before her slit-eyed stare.

"In your place," Susi told him, "I would look nearer home . . . for possible death."

The mayor knew his wife, Susi's dear friend, and was silent.

But in July of 1929, twenty years after she first came to Nagyrev, there occurred an accident that wasn't allowed for in Susi's plans. The Calvinist minister in Tiszakurt made a routine pastorly call on Mrs. Ladislas Szabo. "It's strange," he mused, "how death came alike to your aged father and uncle on the same night, almost in the same moment."

The reminder was too much for grieving Mrs. Szabo. She began to sob and only gradually grew calm enough to brew the pastor a cup of tea.

He returned to his house and his visitor, an old school-mate from Budapest who was a doctor, bothered by a queer taste in his throat. Not many hours later, the sickness seized him. Only the accidental presence of his guest, who had a stomach-pump to hand, saved the pastor's life. Two days later, he and his friend made a sudden, unexplained trip to Szolnok.

Nagyrev was celebrating a half-forgotten saint's day when the gendarmes from Szolnok marched into the village. From woman to woman the police moved, pausing to read an accusation, then clasp steel bracelets over fear-stiffened wrists.

Panic swept the guilty. Women who had not yet been approached began to confess publicly. Others accused their neighbors. All mentioned the name of Susi Olah.

Susi faced Dr. Kronberg, the prosecutor, with the same sleepy-eyed certainty she had known in Budapest twenty years before, when the sight of dying flies struggling on her window sill first showed her the way to power and pleasure. She shrugged the questions off lazily. The doctor knew women. Women were ignorant and foolish; doubtless they accused her because of some grudge.

The doctor agreed. He told her she was free to go home. Wrapped in her black shawl, Susi returned alone to Nagyrev.

She hesitated just outside the village. Then, a half-smile curving her lips, she did what she thought wise. One by one, she called on more than thirty women, spoke briefly in their doorways. Then she went home and made herself comfortable in an oaken armchair.

The great, yellow cat, descendant of twenty other yellow cats that she had petted and fondled, climbed into her lap, turned round and lay purring. Slowly her fingers stroked his fur.

Down the street, women's voices began to scream. Susi sat up, pushed the cat to the floor and waddled to the window. Policemen—she knew instantly that they had secretly and on orders preceeded her back to the village—were entering the houses she had visited. She saw them dragging out a woman here, another there.

During the spring and summer of 1930, thirty-one women went to trial in Szolnok for arsenic poisonings. Five of the accused took their own lives, eleven were sentenced to death, and the remainder given life sentences. These were the ones who murmured, "I did not murder. I did not stab or drown. I only gave a little water from a medicine bottle sold by Susi Olah." She had schooled them well.

Susi herself said nothing. The policeman outside her door behaved with a gallantry she had no right to expect from his sex. He delayed his entry until she finished a little business with a rope stretched in her clothes closet.

Inquisition by Night

She thought: *He doesn't look like a killer.*

S HE AWOKE slowly, consciousness returning in little halting steps like the tread of a blind man over unfamiliar ground. Only half awake like this, she could still hear the voices from

By Wallace Umphrey

her nightmare. *Tell us what you know, Janey. Tell us what he told you before he died. Think, Janey. Tell us everything.*

It was madness. Mr. Peery knew! Insanity was clawing at her brain. You could inherit madness, couldn't you? She lay there in the darkness with her eyes closed. No! It wasn't madness. Her danger was real!

She listened. Out of the darkness of her mind came the sound of the voice. . . beating like a giant fist at her brain. *Tell us everything.* The words came like heavy blows out of the sky. Words; evenly spaced now, measured, like the ticking of a clock, like the beating of a great heart. *What did he tell you, child, before he died?*

"Nothing!" she screamed aloud into the darkness. "He told me nothing!"

Her breath sobbed in her throat. She felt spent. Other sounds crept into her consciousness. She could hear the surf pounding on the beach, the rain rattling against the windows. From out across the wind-swept water came the lonely cry of a sandpiper.

Rain dripped from the eaves to the ground. Drip, drip, drip. A steady rhythm. Danger. . . .Danger. . . . Danger!

She listened for Hugo's snoring from the hearth, and then she remembered that the big dog was dead. It was her turn next. A new sound penetrated her conscious mind. Out in the hall a board creaked. It was Bob and he was home from his night trick on the newspaper in the city. He was her husband. He would love her and protect her. Or would he?

Bob had poisoned Hugo.

Danger. . . . Danger. . . . Danger!

Light footsteps approached. The bedroom door swung open and she could smell tobacco smoke and his damp tweeds. Through her lids, so tightly closed, she could sense the fat wedge of light from the hallway. Her nightmare came back to crowd her mind. *Tell us, Janey.* The footsteps came near the bed and she could stand it no longer. Her eyes sprang open.

Bob was standing beside the bed, bending toward her. She could see him dimly—something upraised in his hand.

A knife!

With a strangled cry, she rolled out of bed beyond his reach. There was a strange warmth in her toes and in her fingers. Her ears felt hot and her scalp prickled. She sneezed violently. Reeling sideways, she clutched a chair for support. She thought: *Why does he want to kill me?*

"Bob!" she cried. "Bob—don't!"

He took a little backward step. His hand holding the knife dropped to his side. His dark eyes looked a little stupid, perplexed, a little unbelieving.

She thought: *He doesn't look like a killer.* And she thought: *He's clever and he's a good actor and he's smart enough to try to cover his tracks.* And then she thought: *Why—why!*

"Don't what?" he asked. "Kitten, I don't understand."

"That knife!" she cried. "It's meant for me!"

He lifted the knife, stared at it. He shook his head in bewilderment and his dark hair fell down over his forehead. She thought wildly: *Why does he have to pretend now?*

She reeled back, crowding against the wall in her thin nightdress. Her eyes fell on the lamp on the bedside table. Bob was still staring stupidly at the knife in his hand. She caught up the lamp, jerked out the plug and flung the lamp at his head. It caught him on the temple and he staggered back against a chest of drawers.

Fleeing around the foot of the bed, she ran outside into the wind and rain and darkness. The low, dripping boughs of a fir tree seemed to clutch at her shoulders like evil hands. She ran along the beach and she could hear the surf and the wind and the voices in her head. Faintly from the house she had just fled she heard the faint but sudden burst of the telephone bell. . . .

THEY had moved here to the beach just three days ago. The housing shortage cooped them up in a stifling one-room apartment in the city, and just the thought of moving into a house at the beach, a real honest-to-goodness house where you had the freedom to really breathe again, was pretty wonderful.

She waited up to tell Bob about it, until two o'clock when he got home from his job.

"A house?" he said guardedly. "What's that?" He shook his dark head. "Never heard of such a thing." Then he grinned. "I'll bite. Just where did we get a house?"

It had been her father's house. She had inherited it. There had been no will. The house seemed to be the sum total of the estate.

"Okay," he said. "Let's move tomorrow."

Some of the excitement faded from her eyes. She shivered a little, remembering. Her father had always been a stranger to her, a grim, brooding, taciturn man. She had really never known him at all.

Her mother died before she was old enough to remember, and her father had always kept her away in boarding schools. Only seldom had she visited him there at the beach. He had always seemed like a man made grim and lonely and bitter by some terrible secret.

She remembered his dying. The hospital had called her. He was lying on his deathbed with a bullet in his brain. He didn't even recognize her, and his rush of words were incoherent. "Vickers!" he gasped. "Don't look at me like that! It was Ransome!" She didn't recognize any of these names.

They told her that her father had tried to kill himself before and now he had succeeded. They said it was a miracle how he had driven himself to the hospital with a bullet in his brain.

"Wait," she said now. "Bob, you never knew my father. He lived there at the beach, alone and lost, for as long as I can remember. There was something—almost evil about him. I shouldn't say that maybe, but we were strangers. He always frightened me."

"Are you trying to tell me that a house could take on some of the character of a guy who lived in it?" He shook his head. "I says it's spinach. I've got imagination, but not that much."

"You don't understand," Janey said desperately. "I—I was always frightened when I visited him."

"Nuts! You were afraid of him, but not of the house. You'll see." His voice leveled. "We'll move tomorrow." Looking at her, he knocked the ashes from his pipe. "It's going to be good for you, Janey. All that stuff they call fresh air. You've been looking sort of run-down lately."

Standing up, all six feet of him uncoiling lazily, he took her in his arms. "Kitten, have I ever told you that I love you?"

They packed the next morning before Bob went away to work. Janey glimpsed herself in a mirror and she remembered what Bob had told her last night. She guessed she did look kind of run-down. There were dark circles under her eyes and she'd lost weight. A few weeks in the country air would fix that!

She smiled to herself, thinking about her fears of last night. A house was just a house. She was an idiot and Bob was right in rushing her away from the city.

"Well, this is it," he had said nailing the cover on the final box. "All packed. I've got to run to work. Kitten, we'll sleep on the floor tonight. First thing in the morning, the moving van will be here."

The next morning Janey was watching

out of the window when a truck arrived. It was a small truck, not big enough for a van. She frowned. A man got out leading the biggest dog she'd ever seen. A Great Dane. She turned from the window and Bob grinned smugly.

"It's for you," he said. "A going-away present. I bought him yesterday. The beach is lonely and I'm away evenings—"

Janey kissed her husband soundly "I'll call him Hugo," she cried gaily.

Then the moving van arrived and everything was work and confusion until finally they were at the beach. Janey had already made friends with Hugo. The Peerys came along just as the van was driving away. Janey knew them slightly. They were the nearest neighbors, a quarter of a mile away. Hugo growled at them, deep in his throat, and Janey had to quiet the big dog.

Mr. Peery was a small, gray man with alert eyes. His wife was plump and red-cheeked. Janey introduced them to Bob. They all sat down amid the welter of furniture and boxes. "I brought along some coffee," said Mrs. Peery as she opened a thermos. Janey found some cups and it was fun.

"I understand you're a doctor," said Bob politely.

Mr. Peery smiled. "Retired."

"Keep an eye on Janey, will you?" asked Bob. "She doesn't look too well. And besides, I work nights."

Both of the Peerys nodded. Mrs. Peery said, "We never had a chance to know her very well. Bill used to talk—" She paused, flushing.

"It's all right," Janey said. William Wright had been her father. "I guess you people were the only friends he ever had."

Mrs. Peery nodded. "We all moved here to the beach at the same time. He was a strange man, Mrs. Rafter. I don't mean to be talking against the dead—but he was always distant with me! He was a

good man, too. Many's the time I've seen him reading out of his Bible. Why, child, it was the only book he ever read!"

After awhile, the Peerys left. It was time for Bob to go to work. He pulled a tiny bottle out of his pocket and set it in a corner of the drain board. He said, "I remembered to get this, kitten. It's ant poison. You always have ants in the country. You be careful of it. Just leave it for the ants. It'll slay 'em."

Janey finally got some semblance of order out of the chaos. It was almost nine o'clock. She listened to the wind and rain. Going to the window, she peered out. It was like black velvet out there, but she could see the fir tree in front of the house. Those were *not* arms reaching out for her, she told herself. Hugo was asleep on the hearth. Suddenly, everything seemed very still, and her fear of last night came back to her. There was evil here! She felt it all around her and she shivered apprehensively.

A knock sounded on the door. Hugo lifted his big head and growled. Janey felt her knees shake a little as she crossed to the door. It was only Mr. Peery.

"I brought some pills, Mr. Rafter," he said, glancing at the dog. "Just take one if you have trouble sleeping. You've had so much excitement today. They're quite harmless."

"They won't hurt me?"

"Of course not!"

Janey said suddenly, "You're a doctor. What was the matter with my father?"

Mr. Peery sighed. "He was a paranoid. This may not mean much to you. Your father suffered from delusions of persecution."

"Can—can it be inherited?"

"Yes. Yes, of course." Mr. Peery's eyes were bright. "But you don't have to be worried about being persecuted."

Mr. Peery went away and Janey sat in front of the fire. She was bone-weary but somehow she didn't feel like sleeping. It was the excitement, she guessed. Although she hadn't eaten since breakfast, she wasn't hungry. She listened to the rain. The walls of the house seemed to shrink in upon her and she was afraid. She shivered. Undressing hurriedly, she took one of the sleepings pills and crawled into bed.

The pattern of the rain on the window pane. . . . a sudden gust of wind. Danger . . . . danger . . . .danger, it whispered. Then sleep. And in this house of evil came the nightmare. . . .

SHE awoke slowly into a sleep-drugged world. Out of the dark void of her nightmare came the voice. *Child, you still haven't remembered the thing we want to know,* it urged. She lay there in the darkness, biting her lip, trying to reassure herself. It had been a dream, she knew, and dreams couldn't hurt you. She heard the wind and the rain. This was real. The other just a nightmare.

You haven't told us yet, Janey.

There in the darkness she trembled. That voice seemed real enough—and deadly. The back of her hand itched and she rubbed it, thinking: *Nettles. There's a patch of nettles outside the house.*

Her feet and hands felt warm. With a shaking hand, she switched on the bed lamp and looked at the clock. It was almost six in the morning.

Where was Bob? He was always home by two. What had happened to him?

She listened now, trying to hear some sound inside the house. . . any sound! The surf breaking monotonously outside gave her no comfort. Here in the house everything was as quiet as the grave. Where was Hugo? He should be snoring in front of the hearth.

Fear gripped her, but she forced herself out of bed and reeled into the living room. Hugo was gone. She called him but the only answer was the wild beating of her heart.

She tried to think. She had left the big dog sleeping in front of the fire. All doors and windows were closed. She thought desperately: *I've got to keep calm, reason things out.*

That didn't help. Maybe she'd let Hugo out before she went to bed. She couldn't remember. Everything was all mixed up.

Where was Bob?

Why was she left alone in this evil house?

She crept back to the bedroom in her bare feet, fright alive in her mind. Hastily she swallowed another sleeping tablet. . . .

Later she awoke with pale daylight in her face. Bob was just getting dressed. For a moment she watched him, pleased with the ripple of muscles along his bare chest and shoulders and the way his dark hair curled above his high forehead. She remembered what Mr. Peery had said. Bob loved her. He was her husband. She was safe now.

And then she remembered the night and the darkness and the voice. The voice . . : the voice that hammered at her out of the void. She looked at the clock and it was only ten in the morning. That meant Bob hadn't had much sleep, even though he looked rested.

He saw that she was awake. "You shouldn't go outside in your bedroom slippers," he said.

That didn't make sense. "What?" she asked.

"Sand on them," he said, picking one up. "See?"

She stared dully. How had the sand got there? Bob went back to buttoning his shirt.

"You got in late," she said suddenly.

"Same time, kitten." He didn't look at her. "Just about two."

For a moment her mind wrestled with the problem of the sand on her slippers.

She gave that up and her gaze sharpened. The night seemed a little hazy now, but she knew the clock had indicated six when she had awakened that time.

"What was it?" she asked. "A poker game?"

He turned, surprised. "Are you nuts?"

She thought dully: *Why is he lying to me?*

The night crowded back into her mind. Absently she rubbed the back of her hand. Bob was watching her. Did he seem changed somehow? Were his eyes watching her strangely?

"Kitten, what's wrong with your hand?"

"Nettles," she said. "Where's Hugo?"

"Golly, I forgot about him!" He looked normal now. "I didn't see him last night when I got home."

Fear possessed her again. She climbed out of bed and stood up, steadying herself against the wall. The strange look came back into Bob's eyes. It didn't matter. She had to find Hugo. That was the important thing. She had to prove to herself that Hugo was all right and everything that had happened was only a bad dream.

"Look at you stagger," Bob said suddenly. "You're drunk!"

She didn't answer. She pulled on her clothing and then ran outside. "Hugo!" she called, running down the steps. She found him dead, lying beside the porch.

"Poisoned," said Bob. "Poor fellow."

They stared each other. Numbly, Janey stumbled back into house. She guessed Bob was doing something about the dog. He came inside, headed for the kitchen.

"LOOK!" He held the bottle of ant poison in one hand. "It's empty." He walked closer, staring down into her eyes. "I don't get it, kitten. What happened last night?"

She wanted to say aloud: "Nothing happened." She wanted desperately to lie. But the nightmare was still too vivid for that. And the truth would sound silly. Maybe she *was* going crazy. You couldn't talk about that, could you, until you were sure?

"Why were you so late?" she asked.

"Don't start that again, for Pete's sake!" He rumpled his dark hair and his face looked strained. He came out of the bedroom with one of the sleeping pills Mr. Peery had given her. "What's this?" he asked.

She told him that much. He looked angry. They stared at each other across a gap of silence that widened and widened until they were miles apart. Bob opened his mouth, swallowed, snapped it shut again.

Janey thought: *He was going to ask me if I could have poisoned Hugo in my sleep. He's thinking about my slippers. How did the sand get there?*

Then she thought wildly: *He did it! He killed Hugo!*

The day passed. There was the steady beat of the rain, everlasting, never ending. Then Bob left for work. Janey was terrified of being left alone, but maybe it was better this way. She tried to eat but food nauseated her. The evil in the house was all around her again, alive and tangible. She was going mad. Finally, in desperation, she took a sleeping pill and drifted off into sleep.

She heard the voice. *Tell us, child. What did he tell you just before he died?*

She tossed and rolled and twisted, but this time she didn't awaken. Then it was morning again.

Bob looked haggard. "What do you know about this Peery guy?" he asked, as soon as Janey opened her eyes.

Sleep-drugged, she said, "Nothing."

"I took one of those sleeping pills into town with me," he told her. "And damned if it wasn't just that, a harmless pill."

"Why should it be anything else?"

"Maybe I'm nuts," Bob said.

She looked at him and he was a stranger. She had never seen him before. She thought: *He's trying to throw the guilt on somebody else.*

"Bob!" she cried. "What's happening to use? It's this house! Oh, Bob, darling, please let's move back to the city!"

His mouth was grim. He shook his head. "No. This house is made of wood and nails and glass and brick. That's all. I'll never believe that evil can be absorbed by a chunk of wood!"

That proved it to her. That proved she was in danger.

The day passed and it was worse than the day before. She was glad to be alone. Daylight faded and it was dark and the fear was back. She walked slowly through the house, touching those things which had been her father's. She found his Bible and picked it up. Holding it like that, she felt a little comforted. She thought: *Why do I think there is evil in this house?*

Her father had been a good man. Mrs. Peery had told her so. There was no evil here. And then with a shock she realized what that meant.

It meant that it was all in her mind. All her fear was just imagination. She was going crazy. No! Her fear was real!

The Bible slipped from her shaking hand. She stooped to pick it up, not conscious of the effort. Something—a piece of paper—had slipped out. She picked it up, a tiny newspaper clipping yellow and brittle with age.

Today a posse returned after an unsuccessful search of the desert for the three bandits who last week staged the daring bank robbery in Nero. One of the bandits, identified as William Vickers, was found dead, a bullet in his head and a gun in his hand, an empty canteen beside him. He was already partly covered by sand. It is assumed that he shot himself rather than die of thirst. None of the loot was found.

A prepared statement from the sheriff's office states that no man can cross the desert on foot and survive. It is assumed that the other two bandits, tentatively identified as Hugh Ransome and Oliver Church, will eventually perish in the heat, although all hope of finding them is abandoned.

And there will be a fourth casualty. It was learned only yesterday that William Vickers picked up a child, presumably his own, before attempting flight across the burning sands. . . .

Her eyes still dazed, Janey put down the Bible with the newspaper clipping on top of it. Two of the names were the same as those mentioned by her father as he lay dying. But it still meant nothing to her.

She thought: *Damn the rain! This house—I can't stand it! Sleep. . . . I'll go to sleep.*

She didn't know which was worse—nightmare-ridden sleep or this deadly wakefulness. Maybe sleep was better. She took another of the sleeping pills.

It seemed to come immediately—the voice. *Tell us what you know, child.* It went on and on, through eternity. And then she was awake and Bob was bending over her with a knife and she was running along the beach in her thin nightdress with the surf pounding in her ears while above it all the voice kept hammering at her brain. . . .

HER fists on the door brought light and shuffling footsteps. Mr. Peery opened the door and she reeled inside, shivering, her thin nightdress soaked.

"Child, child," he said. "What is it?"

"Bob!" she cried. "He's going to kill—"

For a moment she was faint. Mr. Peery poured a small glass of brandy for her. His eyes were alert. "Does he know you came here?"

"I don't know! Probably."

Mr. Peery stood motionless for a moment. Then he ran toward the stairs and returned with a gun. Suddenly he didn't seem like a little man any more.

"You stay here," he said. "I'll go find him. He's too dangerous to have around loose."

Janey shivered. "You won't hurt him?"

"No. No, child."

She sat alone, hearing the slamming of the door . . . still hearing the voices in her head . . . and the wind and rain, still remembering the picture of Bob standing over her with a knife in his hand. She crept to the fire for warmth, poking up the dying embers. She listened but she could hear nothing.

Where was Mrs. Peery? What was happening outside?

It seemed like a long time before Mr. Peery came back. He came in swiftly, closing the door behind him before he turned, drops of rain glistening in his gray hair. There was a bruise on his cheek and his eyes were bright.

Janey put a hand to her mouth. "You didn't—"

"Of course not. I left him trussed up outside."

There hadn't been a shot. Janey knew suddenly that she would have heard it.

She was glad—even though Bob wanted to murder her.

"What shall we do?" she asked piteously.

Mr. Perry turned on the light in the center of the room, pulled a chair close to her. He sat down, stared into her eyes. She could see the outline of the gun in his pocket. His eyes seemed to glitter with a frenzied light.

"That depends," he said. "We'll have to talk. Child, tell me what he told you before he died."

Janey went rigid. She stared at Mr. Peery in horror. That voice, measured and slow, like the beating of a great heart, like the ticking of a clock. It was the voice in her dreams!

It couldn't be and yet it was! She didn't know how. She started to slide out of her chair but his firm hand held her. She stared at the bulge in his pocket. His eyes glittered madly. Why, Mr. Peery . . . *he was insane!*

Her mind was like a giant pinwheel ready to explode. Somehow Mr. Peery had talked to her in her sleep, had imposed his voice into her dreams. He had killed Hugo because the great dog didn't

trust him. He had set the clock to confuse her, so that she'd think she was going crazy. He'd put sand on the soles of her bedroom slippers so she would think she might be walking in her sleep, so she'd be afraid she might have killed Hugo herself. He was one of the three bandits who had robbed the bank—and her father had been another.

Only it wasn't her father. Her father had died in the desert almost twenty years ago. The man named Oliver Church had taken her and raised her as his daughter.

Mr. Peery was Hugh Ransome and he had killed her real father back there on the desert when she was a baby, so that the bank loot would be split only two ways. Somehow, he and Oliver Church had fought their way to freedom. Oliver Church had taken her and changed his name, but that crime of long ago had preyed on his mind. That was why he wanted to kill himself—a guilt complex.

With sudden strength, she twisted out of Mr. Perry's grasp. His hands fumbled for her but she twisted away. He stumbled after her as she ran outside.

Hard sand was under her bare feet. She could hear him panting behind her. The gun in his pocket—he wouldn't use until he had to.

There was the wind and the rain and the darkness. But the voice of her nightmare . . . it was gone now. Darkness was a welcome thing now. But it wouldn't save her. He would catch her eventually. He was already cutting down the distance between them. She felt him claw at her shoulder.

Then something else came out of the darkness and there was a heavy grunt and a curse. Mr. Peery was down in the sand with somebody on top of him.

Bob! Bob had got away. . . .

* * *

"What he gave you," Bob told her later, "was undoutedly pentothal sodium.

It was given to you while you were asleep, knocked out by sleeping pills. Don't think I'm going scientific on you all of a sudden—"

He grinned and rubbed his wrists. She could see the marks of them left by the rope.

"You see, kitten, I've been talking to a doctor friend of mine. I handed him the symptoms—the hot feet and hands, the sneezing and reeling, the itch on the back of your hand, which is where the stuff was administered—and he decided that's what it was. It's a drug used by psychiatrists to aid a patient in trying to recollect memories stored in the subconscious mind. So help me, kitten, I really thought you were drunk!"

Janey shuddered.

"That clipping tipped me off, too. Peery had to know if your alleged father babbled any of the truth before he died. Such a truth floating around would be damned dangerous to him, and so he had to know.

"And if you think you're crazy, all you have to do is watch Peery in action and you'll know you're as sane as sunshine! I don't know, maybe he's not crazy. But through the years he managed to build up a potent bunch of fright and guilt complexes!"

He looked down at his wrists. "His prints were even on the bottle of ant poison. I took it downtown with me to have it checked. That's what the phone call was about when you rushed out."

"But—that knife in your hand," Janey murmured.

Bob laughed. "I was in the kitchen when you groaned. Naturally, since I'm a good husband, I wondered what was the matter. Naturally, since I love you dearly, I rushed into the bedroom to see . . . still holding the knife. Can't a guy make a sandwich when he comes home from work hungry without being accused of trying to murder his wife?"

SHOCKERS AHEAD

FROWNING, Dixon peered at the dark, isolated Parke cottage. The glint in his squinting eyes told me he, too, knew Cynthia Parke was in that deserted beach cottage. So, I'd damned well better face the fact—this slinking little newshound knew more about Cyn, somehow, than I did.

He looked back, lifting his sly black eyes to mine with a cynical shrug. "Do you really need to be told what your Cynthia is doing, Mr. Reece? If so, let me refer you to tomorrow's *Press.* Meanwhile I might mention one angle. Tonight's the first time you've tailed her around—but I started it three nights ago. On a hunch. A newsman's hunch. One of the kind that the instant it hits you you know it's got to be right. It hasn't led me much anywhere until I stole a ride out here in your trunk. But now I've got the feeling that tonight's the payoff."

No matter how deftly Cyn might be two-timing me in that dark cottage, I couldn't let Dixon splash it out in headlines. I couldn't let him hurt old Judge Parke, nor would I welcome any sabotage on my own career. Dixon had to be stopped.

That's why I jumped Dixon—with no punches pulled. He whirled away, lashing out his foot at my stomach. When I went down, he stumbled out across the night-shrouded dunes toward the Parke Cottage on the bay shore. I pulled myself up and started after him, reeling like a drunk. I was still twenty yards away when he reached the door.

His hand clenched the knob and he was startled to find the illicit door unbolted. In a frenzy to keep out of my reach and at the same time to pin down his front-page dirt, he sidled inside.

The door had not yet began to close behind him when the shots blasted out.

Three shots in swift succession. The flame of the gun could be seen at the nearest windows and at the open door—three copper-red flashes. The reports seemed tremendous bursts in the stillness of the night-wrapped shore.

I stumbled closer to the open door. Now a steady light had appeared—the shaft of a flashlight aimed from inside the room. It shone down on Dixon as he lay there on the floor just inside the door. Three holes in his belly were leaking blood.

The light was gripped in one of Cynthia Parke's hands, and in the other she clenched the automatic—and both those fine, delicate, patrician hands of hers were as steady as the finger of Death.

A very effective job of murder, this—fast and thorough, as done by my tender bride-to-be.

Lying there inert with the blood seeping out of him, Dixon looked as dead as he would ever get—but he wasn't quite dead enough to suit Cyn in her fury. Suddenly the gun in her hand let out its shattering fire again. Twice. With her face strained into lines of sheerest hatred and her fine teeth gleaming in the oval of her tight-pulled lips, she stepped closer to send two more bullets smashing squarely into the hollow of the corpse's gaping mouth . . . .

The complete story of Reece and his aristocratic and blood-thirsty Cynthia Parke will be told by Frederick C. Davis in his novel—"I'll Marry a Killer" in the next issue of SHOCK—Out June 2nd.

Blood of

... ♦ ♦ ♦

Exotic captive of a power-mad barbarian, Latmini bartered a blood-soaked Buddhist treasure for the wares of a ruthless merchant of death.

CHAPTER ONE

Beautiful Pawn

ONE HUNDRED times during the long dream-like trip across the Pacific she had remembered the slow words of Sakna Kahn, remembered the fanatic brightness of his eyes, the pain of his lean brown fingers bruising the flesh of her arm.

When the freighter rolled heavily in the long blue swells of the Pacific, she spread her robe on the rough canvas of the hatch cover, stretched out in the rude warm touch of the tropic sun, dressed in the brief two-piece sun suit she had bought in the lobby of the Taj in Bombay.

She shut her eyes against the florid sun, and the gentle rise and fall of the vessel rocked her with a soft, almost sensual motion.

She was tall, taut, clean-limbed but in the wideness of her mouth, the limber way she carried herself, there was a hint of something elemental, almost savage.

Twice she had felt a shadow across her face during the early part of the trip, two days out of Bombay, and had looked up to see the square, pasty face of Gibson, the ship's second officer. He had a habit of speaking out of lips that barely moved and of never looking into her eyes.

But there had been an answer for Gibson. A slim and delicate answer. Six inches of delicately engraved steel blade with mottled jade hilt. Sakna Kahn had given it to her. It was the last thing he had given her, pressed hurriedly into her hand as he helped her down into the little craft that took her out to the ship.

Sakna Kahn had remembered every detail. He was oddly powerful in political circles. There had been no difficulty getting permission—permission for a Burgh-

the Vixen ··· ◆ ◆ ◆

Exciting Shock-Mystery Novelette

By John D. MacDonald

"The knife is for you—" she answered in a half-whisper.

er girl to visit the states on a temporary visa.

But she was not like other Burgher girls. Not like her Anglo-Indian cousins in Hindustan and Pakistan, the girls with the blue shade in the deep tan of their skin, the purplish look to their fingernails. Those girls fled from the sun.

She, Latmini Perez, her skin the shade of a jigger of coffee in a liter of milk, could doze in the bright sun, the small beads of perspiration gleaming amid the transparent down that covered her rounded arms and legs. She had much Dutch and Portugese blood in her, very little of the blood of Singh, the lion.

That was one of the reasons Sakna Kahn had selected her. There had been no chance of refusal. Refusal would have meant being dragged, some dark night, into a waiting car and taken out through the warm night, past the sleeping villages beyond the Victoria Bridge and left to rot in the jungle. . . .

She remembered Sakna Kahn's words: "It is a very simple plan—so it won't fail. But you may have been seen talking with me. Our enemies are many, and they are clever. They will not expect our plan to be this simple. I will keep your passage as secret as possible. And yet they will find out. If you are careless, they will take you, and there will be many ways in which they will encourage you to speak of this plan. Before you leave, I will give you something which will spare you such torment. Strike deep!"

His words had made no sense to her until the knife was slipped into her hand. Already it had been of use. When Gibson walked up to stare at her on the third day, she had plucked the knife from under the edge of the robe and slid the point of it along the steel deck near the hatch cover. It had made a small grating noise.

Gibson had licked his lips. "What's that for?"

"The knife is for you—if needs be," she answered in a half-whisper. Gibson left hurriedly.

There was but one other passenger. An American, with face stained and blotched with disease, returning home to die. He seldom left his cabin.

And that was the way Latmini Perez wished the trip to be. Alone. Time to think. Time to remember. Time to grow accustomed to fear.

As she remembered Sakna Kahn's words, she reached with her right hand and, with gentle fingertips, touched the thin white ridge of scar tissue that marred the clear skin above her knee. She frowned. The scar would always be there. There should be a way to make Sakna Kahn pay for that blemish. Pay in blood, as she had payed.

Yes, the plan was simple. So simple that it should succeed. If she did not become careless.

After customs inspection and verification of her papers in the Port of Los Angeles, she left the ship and went directly to the railroad station Sakna Kahn had mentioned. As he had ordered, she made no attempt at all to see if she was being followed.

She checked her two suitcases at the station, caught a taxi and went to the heart of the shopping section. There she bought with the money he had given her, several new dresses, a light suit, a hat, underthings, nylons, accessories. She bought a bag for them, a lightweight expensive suitcase.

She left the clothes she had purchased in Bombay behind, and wore her new things. Carrying the bag with her, she went to a movie, and left ten minutes later by the side door. She took a taxi out to Wiltshire and had the driver let her off on a corner. When a bus stopped, she waited until the last possible moment before boarding it. She was certain then that she wasn't followed. With the change of clothes, she had become an American girl, with an excellent tan, and an interesting trace of something foreign in her manner, and particularly in her speech.

Forsaking the bags she had checked, she took a Pacific Electric train to San Bernadino and there transferred to a major railroad headed East. Six hundred miles later she changed from coach to pullman.

She slept, lulled by the clattering and rocking of the pullman car. In her sleep her slim fingers touched the mottled jade hilt of the slim dagger. With the blade sheathed, it was taped to her side, hilt down. Her body warmed the jade.

LATMINI PEREZ shut herself in a telephone booth in the Pennsylvania Station. Sakna Kahn had made her memorize the number. It took her several moments to figure out the alphabetical and numerical combination on the dial.

A woman answered, her voice high and impatient. "Yes? What is it?"

"Badla lena," she answered, saying the Hindi phrase meaning 'revenge.' To have come so many thousand miles through the watchfulness of the enemy in order to say these few words into the black, chipped mouthpiece. . . .

"Oh! I see. Wait a moment, please." The line was silent. Latmini took a deep, shuddering breath.

A man came on the line. "Listen carefully. You can't come here. Go to the Hotel Arnot on West Fiftieth. There will be a reservation for you there, made in the name of Janice Walters. Go to your room and stay there. Be careful. Open the door for the man who will say, 'Are you ready yet, Miss Walters?' Is that clear?"

"Yes."

The line clicked, went dead. She stepped out of the booth, picked up the suitcase and walked quickly back into the waiting room, reassured by the dense crowds and yet afraid of who might be in those crowds.

The Arnot was in a dusty brown building, the lobby entrance dim and bleak as compared with a garish door to the left over which sputtering neon announced, *The Arnot Grill—Music by Al Denees.*"

The desk clerk was a blond young man with pointed features. He looked approvingly at her as she said, "You have a reservation for me? Janice Walters."

He placed the registration card in front of her. "Yes, we do, Miss Walters. But we can't give you a single. Will a suite be okay?"

"Excellent."

She signed, the clerk tapped the desk bell and gave the key to the hop who hurried over. He picked up her suitcase, led the way to the elevator and stepped aside as she walked in. Eighth floor. Thick rugs, badly worn on the corridor floor. White carved moulding and deep aqua walls. Thick, soft silence and the odor of dust.

"To your right, Miss."

Eight oh nine and eight eleven at the end of the corridor. He clicked on the overhead lights, and the small sitting room was cheerless, the furniture arranged geometrically, the tapestry upholstery stained with oil from the hair of the countless people who had sat there.

The bedroom was in contrast, the walls refinished in pale gray, the furniture new, modern, inescapably cheap.

The hop said, "They're redecorating. In this layout the bedroom's all done but they haven't touched this sitting room yet."

She wasn't used to the currency. She handed him the largest of her silver coins and it seemed to be adequate. "Call the desk if you want anything," he said, let himself out. She affixed the chain across the door, hurried to the bedroom and did the same with the bedroom door which opened on the corridor. Then she slipped the taped knife into her sleeve.

On impulse, she turned off the lights, stood by the wide windows and looked down into the honking, confusing traffic of Fiftieth Street. For the first time in many days, she felt almost relaxed. With relaxation came reaction. She walked into the bedroom, sat listlessly on the edge of the bed, the tip of her cigarette making a subdued red spot in the darkness. When the cigarette was done, she stubbed it out and lay back on the bed. The traffic noise was a vast, throbbing lullaby. . . .

She started violently, suddenly aware of the tapping at her door. There was a bitter taste in her mouth. Her sleep had been sound. She stood up so quickly that she wavered dizzily. In the sitting room, she turned on the floor lamp and a table lamp and arranged her hair quickly as she walked to the door.

"Who is there?"

"Are you ready yet, Miss Walters?"

She slipped the chain off and opened the door. The stocky man came in, his hat in his hand. He had a violently florid complexion, hair so blond as to be almost white, his eyebrows and small mustache startling against the veined red of his skin. His eyes were pale, watery blue, quite vague—but she got the impression that those eyes saw all that was necessary to see. He was very well dressed.

He closed the door behind him, slipped the chain back in the slot, and took off his topcoat, threw topcoat and hat on the frayed couch and sat down heavily in the nearest chair, looking at her with evident approval.

"I'm Roger," he said, as though that one word explained everything.

"Roger? I don't—"

"Of course you don't, my dear." His voice had the clipped, flat accent of a Lord Haw Haw. "It isn't necessary that you know." He looked at her intently, his

eyes ranging from ankle to throat. She backed away and sat down. "A very nice job of selection by our friend, Sakna," he said.

"Against my will," she said.

Roger laughed. "Of course, my dear. No one willingly does this sort of thing, you know. That is, unless they happen to be psychopathic. I would assume that you are—quite normal."

"What is the next step?" she said.

"You will tell me every detail of your instructions," he said quietly.

She shook her head. "No. I cannot."

His face turned a deeper shade and his eyes narrowed. "May I ask why not?"

"Part of my instructions are to tell no one."

He smiled. "Oh, but those instructions came from Sakna Kahn. Here you are under my jurisdiction, my dear. I countermand his orders."

"I won't accept the change," she said firmly. "It is all very well for you to ignore him, but I have to go back there. You don't. As long as I have to go back and report to him, I will do exactly what he told me to do."

His anger faded. "You are stubborn, my dear. Very well, then. If you won't, you won't. At least we've done part of our job. We've put you in the same hotel where Karl Ehrlich is staying. Sakna Kahn at least managed to tell us that much of your mission."

"Ehrlich is—here!" she gasped.

"Certainly! You'll know him by sight?"

"Sakna Kahn had one picture. A poor one, cut from a Berlin newspaper from before the war."

"He hasn't changed. He's tall, heavy through the shoulders. Coarse features. He is very mild in action, quite courtly in fact. He has a—shall we say—pronounced regard for the fair sex."

"Sakna Kahn knew that when he—selected me."

Roger smiled. "I assume that Sakna Kahn has the usual safeguards to guarantee your obedience?"

She remembered the look in Sakna Kahn's eyes when he had said to her, "Remember, my dear, you have two younger sisters. Any deviation from your instructions would be unfortunate. We would have to pay them a visit. Your family plantation near Ratnapura is quite isolated, is it not?"

"Yes," she said weakly to Roger. "My obedience is beyond question."

"He is a clever man. But so is Ehrlich. It takes a clever man to get a clean bill of health from the War Crimes people when you have Ehrlich's background. I must be leaving. You have the number. In case of trouble, telephone again."

HE PICKED up his coat and hat. She followed him to the door. At the door he turned, smiling at her, twirling the hat in his hand. Suddenly the hat smashed up at her face, the room swung like a giant pendulum and there was a touch of fire along the line of her jaw. She felt herself topple toward the floor, but she couldn't feel the impact of landing on the floor. She fell endlessly. . . .

Light stung through her eyelids. She moaned and put her arm across her eyes. From far away Roger said, "Ah, awake again, I see."

She blinked at him. He sat in his shirtsleeves looking at her. She was on the couch. Her jaw hurt. She touched her fingertips to it.

"There will be no mark," he said, "if that's what you're worried about. I masked my fist with my hat."

Under cover of her arm, she reached gently with the fingers of her other hand, found to her dismay that her sleeve was unbuttoned, the jade knife gone.

"Your plaything is on the bureau," he said. "I took the liberty. I thought you might be dangerously angry."

She sat up dizzily, the pain throbbing along the lean line of her jaw. "Why did you?" she whispered hoarsely.

"An elementary precaution. Your little gift for Ehrlich would have been taken if you had had it here. If I could take it, Ehrlich could take it. I assure you, my dear, that you have been carefully searched. I trust you left it in a safe place?"

He smiled with his lips alone. The vague blue eyes had glints of anger.

"I don't believe you, of course," she said.

"That is of no interest to me."

"Had you found what you sought, Roger, you would have been gone by the time I awakened."

"Possibly," he said casually.

"I want to laugh at you," she said. "You have made me feel good. Very good. I was foolish. I thought that Sakna Kahn and the ones like him—you, for example—were selfless fanatics. It is a pleasure to find you are a common thief. It makes all of you less formidable."

He stood up and slowly slipped into his suitcoat, smiling down at her as he buttoned it. "One round for you, my dear. It is like a mathematical equasion. Had I won, you would have been proven a poor one for Sakna Kahn to have sent." He picked up his coat and hat again and hurriedly let himself out. She walked over to the door and replaced the chain.

As she was getting dressed, she ordered her dinner. It was too late to go out alone. When she had finished, she pushed the cart out into the hallway, locked her door and glanced at her watch. Nearly eleven. She thought vaguely of calling Ehrlich, even went so far as to rest her hand lightly on the phone. The idea was poor, she realized, and she was motivated by the urge to get the business over with quickly.

She forced herself to relax. She sat in the darkened room for a time, watching the night silhouettes of the buildings of central Manhattan. She went to bed.

The tapping at the door was insistent. It had worked itself into her dreams before awakening her. In her dreams she was crouched in the heavy dust of a Ceylonese village street. On the far edge of the jungle a machine gun made an odd sleepy noise.

She sat up in the darkness, her palms moist. The tapping sounded again. She stepped into her slippers, padded over to the door and said, close to the panel, "Who is it?"

A woman's voice, oddly familiar, spoke: "Let me come in, please." Something of panic and something of despair was in the voice.

"Who are you?"

"I'm a friend of Roger's. Please. Quickly!"

Leaving the chain on, she opened the door and looked cautiously out. A young woman with heavy facial bones, brown hair, smart clothes stood outside. "Hand me your purse through the crack in the door," Latmini said.

Quickly the girl pushed the purse through, Latmini shut the door, unclasped the purse, looked quickly inside. She snapped it shut, took off the chain and opened the door. The girl came in hurriedly and Latmini locked the door behind her.

Latmini clicked on the bright overhead lights. They stood for an awkward moment, looking at each other inquisitively.

"It is very late. Won't you sit down?" Latmini said.

The girl sat on the edge of the couch in a posture of strain. "Who are you?" Latmini asked.

"Wanda Dziemansek," the girl said. "It means nothing to you, I know. I talked to you before. I answered the phone

when you called. I couldn't come earlier. I—I love Roger Darron."

"I don't see how that can possibly interest me," Latmini said.

"I know how he is," Wanda said. "It has happened before. I will not let it happen again. When he came to see me, he beat me. I knew then that you are beautiful. He beats me when he likes someone else. He drank a great deal and fell asleep. He will not notice that I am gone."

Latmini frowned. "I don't understand all this."

The girl stood up suddenly. She began to pace back and forth. She changed suddenly from a rather stolid-looking brown-haired girl into something of fire and ice and fury. "I tell you that this will not happen again. I, Wanda Dziemansek, will prevent it. Sure, he took me out of a D. P. camp near Munich—but it doesn't matter anymore. I will not wait patiently for him to come back to me again. I am grateful to him no longer."

"I have no interest whatsoever in your Roger Darron."

"It makes no difference. If he likes you, he will find a way. I know how it is done. He knows things about you. Oh, he is very clever." She mimicked his tone: "My deah Miss Walters. You would hate to have me advise the authorities of your real reason for being here, wouldn't you? There will be no need to do that—"

"But isn't he, as a go-between for illicit sales of arms and ammunitions, as vulnerable as anyone else?" Latmini asked.

"There is no evidence against him. None! And he has taken out his first papers. He is better protected than you others who only visit."

"But why do you come here to tell me this nonsense?" Latmini asked.

Wanda tapped her chest. "Because this time it will be different. This time I will go to the authorities and I will tell them why Ehrlich has come here. I will tell which U. N. delegates have been contacted by Ehrlich. I will tell them why Roger Darron has received word from Sakna Kahn. I will expose the whole stinking mess. You think of what I have told you when Roger comes to you with one of his—so delicate proposals. You hear me!"

"Wait a moment, Miss Dziemarsek. I want to ask you—"

"There is nothing more to say to you. I despise you, Miss Walters, or whatever your name is. I could spit into your face! I have seen war, Miss Walters. I have seen the bombs land on the villages. I have seen children with half their faces blown away crawling through the dirt and crying for someone no longer there. Let me go."

"But I don't—"

"You and your kind want it all to come back again. Leave Roger Darron alone!"

There was nothing more to say. Latmini Perez let the girl out, shut the door behind her. Latmini felt emotionally exhausted. She went back to bed but she could not sleep. She thought of Roger Darron's vague eyes, of his florid face. Obviously, if he was able to gain the release of Wanda from a D. P. camp, he must have been in a position of some authority. She wondered if Roger Darron would do as Wanda believed he would.

Suddenly she sat bolt upright, her heart pounding. If Wanda went to the authorities, the entire plan would fail. With Darron out of the way, no one would be able to tell Sakna Kahn exactly what had happened quickly enough. Quickly enough to prevent what Kahn had threatened if Latmini failed to carry out her instructions. Kahn would believe that Latmini Perez had betrayed him.

She thought for a time of the towering hills of Ratnapura, of the neat rows of the clipped tea bushes that marched over the irregular high fields, of the warm taste of arrack and honey. She muffled the sound of her weeping with the corner of the blanket. . . .

CHAPTER TWO

Salesman of Death

SHE managed to smile at the man behind the desk as she said. "You see, it would be very awkward if it turned out to be someone else. But I believe that I know him. If you would please point him out to me. Mr. Ehrlich. When he comes through the lobby." She let him see the five imprint on the folded bill she held. She made her smile warmer. "But he must not know, you understand."

"Perfectly, Miss Walters." The folded bill was whisked off with a furtive motion. Suddenly the desk clerk lowered his voice. "He's coming toward the desk now." There was a glass panel, a mirror, in one of the columns behind the clerk. Latmini glanced into it, saw a man in a neatly cut gray suit, a folded topcoat over his arm. He smiled at the clerk, tossed his key onto the top of the desk and walked toward the lobby door.

"Is he the one you know?" the clerk asked eagerly.

Latmini frowned. "I do not know. It has been so many years. Thank you." She turned away. Karl Ehrlich was bigger than she had guessed. A full six foot two or three and very broad across the shoulders. He moved with a quick light step—the step of a trained athlete, in spite of the fact that he was close to forty.

Ehrlich stood just inside the lobby door, working his arms into his topcoat, staring out at the crowds on the sidewalk. She wondered how it could best be done. Of course, she could always walk up and say, "I wish to talk to you, Herr Ehrlich."

But then there was the danger that he would be alarmed by the blunt approach, feel her so lacking in discretion that he would be afraid to make any sort of deal with her. . .

With sudden decision, she walked by him, pulled open the heavy door and stepped out. She stopped too close to the door and, as she saw it closing, she moved just enough to catch the edge of her coat in the door. She turned, pretending awkwardness, saw him loom up through the glass, pull the door back. "Allow me, please," he said in a gentle voice, a curiously soft voice for so large a man.

He looked at the edge of her coat, bent and touched the soiled spot with a manicured finger. "I do not believe it is torn at all. You are lucky."

"Thank you. If you had not come along, I probably would have torn it trying to pull away."

She smiled up into his face, saw the sudden quickening of interest. "Excuse my boldness," he said. "You are not American, no?"

"Ceylonese. Would you have guessed?"

"No, I would have said Egyptian, possibly Turkish."

She made a face and they both laughed. She said, "You are not an American either. I would say German. Possibly Austrian."

"You are very clever," he said. "Ah, there is a taxi. What way are you going, Miss—"

"Walters. Janice Walters. That is an Anglicised version of my name. I was going to waste an hour looking in shop windows and then I was going to find a place to have lunch. Perhaps you can tell me where I can best waste my hour?"

He bowed and said, "I am delighted to know you, Miss Walters. My name is Ehrlich. Karl Ehrlich." He glanced at his watch. "It is now eleven. If you will permit me, I will be happy to take you to a very pleasant place for lunch. We can go there now, if you wish, and talk about this

fabulous city we are visiting over sherry or cocktails."

She peered at him with a burlesque of suspicion. "You are reputable, Herr Ehrlich?"

He solemnly raised his right hand. "I am a pillar of any community I happen to be in, Miss Walters."

He assisted her into the taxi and directed the driver to take them to a small French restaurant on East Sixty-fourth. There was an awkward silence for a few moments after the cab started up and then he began to talk very charmingly about his first visit to New York City back in 1927 when he knew no English. He soon had her laughing. He used his powerful well-kept hands along with his conversation, using deft gestures to illustrate the little stories he told.

Fifteen minutes after they had entered the restaurant and sat down at a discreet little table in a corner of the lounge, they were evident friends. She noticed that there was no one close enough to them to overhear. He had stopped talking for a moment and was looking at her with obvious approval, his eyes glowing.

She looked into his eyes and said, "Herr Ehrlich, I have come many thousand miles to see you. It is understood that you have certain merchandise for sale."

The glow went out of his eyes, but his lips kept the same easy smile. The brown eyes became as dull and expressionless as stones. He said slowly, "I must be growing fat and unwary. You have been clever."

"I understand that your syndicate will not deal with those who are not clever."

"That is quite right. Did you lie to me about your being Ceylonese?"

"No."

"What is your right name?"

"Must you know that?"

"Do not lie this time. I must know it and it will be necessary for me to check back and see that you are what you claim to be."

"My name is Latmini Perez." She smiled, thinking to make him less cautious. "My friends call me Sitara at times. It means 'star' in Hindustani."

For a moment the glow came back into his eyes. "Star? That is nice. The name 'Stella' means star. May I call you that?"

"I'll have a hard time keeping track of my names. Latmini, Sitara, Stella, Janice."

He became suddenly cautious. "You have not handled this type of mission before?"

"Never."

"Why do you do it at this time?"

"I could lie to you, Karl Ehrlich, and tell you of some inner yen for adventure. I will not lie. I am doing this because harm will come to ones I love if I do not do it."

"In the end, my dear, that is the best way. It was proven during the days of the Third Reich. The most loyal servants are those who have everything to lose, including their lives."

"You do not have to check back to Ceylon. A man in New York can vouch for me, I am sure."

"Who is he?"

"I must trust you, Herr Ehrlich. But there is something I must check. Suppose I merely tell you that the initials of this man are R. D. and that he has a red face."

"Roger Darron is a fool, Stella. I have refused to deal with him further. I have told myself that I will deal with no one again where he is concerned."

She felt a quick rush of alarm. Her voice hoarsened as she said, "But you will not apply that rule to me?"

He looked at her for long moments, licked his heavy lips and said, "You will be the last one."

"Thank you," she breathed.

He glanced around, lowered his tone and said, "I will make another exception. I will be careless and foolish. In return for this concession I make you, I will expect that you will make similar concessions when the opportunity presents itself."

She smiled. "We are without witnesses, of course. And you will probably say nothing specific. So the concessions are something I will have to think about."

HE LAUGHED, almost silently. "Stella, my dear, you have wasted years in not taking up this sort of thing earlier. After this is over, maybe there will be a place in our organization where—"

"After this is over," she said firmly.

"Of course. One thing at a time. You must understand that at the present time the demands on our syndicate are rather heavy. Our shipments have gone out regularly to Palestine, India, China, Burma, the Dutch possessions. But our stocks are now slim. Tell me, will the merchandise we supply be used by trained people?"

"No. It will be used by people who have not been permitted to handle such things for generations."

"Open or guerilla warfare?"

"First guerilla warfare. Sabotage."

"How many men do you hope to have engaged in this enterprize?

"It is said that there should be about five thousand—to begin with. They will capture other merchandise as the fighting goes on."

"When should shipment be made?"

"As soon as possible. The merchandise is to be crated as truck parts and consigned to a name in Colombo. I will give you his name after arrangements are made."

"Deals of this sort are cash in advance."

"We cannot give you cash."

"Then there will be no deal."

"Wait! We can give you something that

is as good as cash. Possibly better. We can deliver it to any spot you designate."

Ehrlich shrugged. "We will need more data than what you have given me. Can you set a value on this something you talk about?"

"Half a million dollars. Minimum valuation."

He smiled. "Do not say that figure with such awe, Stella. We deal in many millions. Once shipment costs are taken out, you leave us ninety dollars with which to equip each of the five thousand you speak of. That is very little. For what you say, we can equip three thousand with our merchandise. And, of course, give you a supply of materials for the sabotage phase. Three thousand rifles of an obsolete type. Forty sub-machine guns. Thirty rounds for each rifle. One thousand rounds for each automatic weapon. Five hundred pounds of plastic explosive with caps and fuses. Three hundred grenades. Nothing more."

"They were very anxious for pistols."

"They are in demand. They cost more than the rifles. Rifles would be as good for your purposes, particularly if your people aren't trained. This is not an offer, however. This is what you might get, provided you could pay cash in advance."

"My instructions are to ask you this: Will you transmit the order to your people and have the items crated, but not stenciled? Then I will take, to any place you say, this item I speak of and you can see its value."

Karl Ehrlich was silent for long seconds. He rubed his massive chin and said, "I like you, Stella. I will agree to that— even though the others will be cross with me."

"What guarantee of performance can I get from you, Mr. Ehrlich?"

"Call me Karl. You can get no guarantee. I can only tell you this. Any failure on our part to fulfill on a promise makes it more difficult in the future to get the prices we ask."

"That is a very small crumb of comfort," she said. "I told you that persons I care for will be hurt, if anything goes wrong, Karl."

He touched her hand with surprising gentleness. "Nothing will go wrong, Stella. Nothing at all."

"Where must I make delivery of this item I have spoken of?" Latmini asked him.

"I will tell you that after I find out more about you."

"Have your people contact Sakna Kahn."

"We know who he is. That will be done."

She wanted to pull her hand away from his, but she knew that it was not time to reveal her feeling . She smiled at him. She remembered the girl who had come to her room. Possibly Karl Ehrlich would find some way of preventing trouble from that direction. It was so obviously not his style to kill, but rather to persuade, that she considered it quite safe to say:

"You called Roger Darron a fool. He is more than that. A girl came to me last night and told me that she had gathered enough information from Roger so as to make a great deal of trouble for all of us if Roger once again walks out on her. She was afraid that Roger was too interested in me. She mentioned your name, said that she knew which U. N. delegates you were contacting."

Karl Ehrlich took his hand away slowly, looked down at the clean nails. His lips barely moved as he said, "Indeed? That is very interesting."

"You know how much all this means to me in a personal way, Karl. It would be a shame if you and I were to get along beautifully, and yet have the entire thing spoiled by this troublesome woman's jealousy."

"She is a Pole, I believe."

"I don't know. Her name is Wanda Dziemansek. I have the telephone number of the apartment where she is staying at present."

"I know where it is. You realize, of course, that there would have been no need for you to leave Ceylon if Darron were trustworthy?"

"I had imagined that that could be the case."

He glanced at his watch. "We must hurry. I have an appointment." He snapped his fingers loudly and the waiter came hurrying over.

He stepped out of the taxi at the entrance to the hotel. With the taxi door still open, he stood and looked down at her, the afternoon sun bright on his face. "I will see you tonight," he said. It was not a question.

Latmini looked at him steadily.

"If you wish."

"At seven thirty. I will telephone you in your room. Until then, Stella. Do not worry."

She looked up into his face, thinking of how each individual feature was blameless in itself, and yet the effect of the whole was one of brutality and ruthlessness. Karl Ehrlich, salesman of death. There was an air of inevitability about him, a courteous and smiling doom.

She shuddered as the taxi drove away, turned quickly and went through the lobby to the elevators.

AT SEVEN she stepped out of her bath. She hurriedly slipped on the dark green dress she had bought in Los Angeles.

It was a lightweight wool, and it pleasantly exaggerated the slimness of her waist, the long clean lines of her throat. She lit a cigarette and stood at the window. The cars had turned on their lights

and the people on the sidewalks walked leisurely.

The knock on the door came at seven twenty-five. Having expected the loud ring of the phone, she was momentarily startled, and then realized that Karl Ehrlich had decided to come up rather than call.

Affixing a smile on unwilling lips, she unfastened the chain and swung the door wide. A strange young man walked in, smiling and unflustered. He was tall, almost as tall as Ehrlich, but he had none of Karl's solidity. This man looked wiry and alert. He had a frank, smiling face, friendly eyes and a scrubbed look.

"I'm afraid you have the wrong room," she said quickly.

He pushed the door shut. "Not at all, Miss Walters. Not at all." He didn't take his hat off, merely shoved it so far back that a lock of red-brown hair fell across his forehead. He had freckles across his nose and a deep scar near the corner of his mouth.

He sat down on the couch, tucked a cigarette in the corner of his mouth and lit it. He looked at her calmly and with approval. She saw that his eyes were brown like Karl's. But not as wise as Karl's. Younger. More naive. She suddenly felt completely capable of handling this friendly young American.

"Sit down, Miss Walters. You look uncomfortable. Pretty dress."

"You'll have to tell me what it is that you want," she said, unsmiling and firm. With a lazy motion he reached into his hip pocket, pulled out a wallet and flapped it open. She saw the silver gleam of the badge, the bright glint of blue enamel.

"Lady, you are entertaining the law. Sit down, honey."

Abruptly she sat. "On second thought," he said, "suppose you show me some identification." His voice was still warm and friendly.

Her mind racing madly, she walked over to her suitcase, unlocked it and took her passport out and carried it over to him.

He glanced at her and at the picture. "Latmini, huh? Is that the way you say it? Latmini Perez. Maybe you don't write so good. On the register it looks like Janice Walters of Los Angeles."

She managed a smile. "There is a man here who would pester me, Mr.—"

"Mr. Joe Harrigan. Now tell me about this man and how he'd bother you."

"Well, he's just a man. What difference does it make, Mr. Harrigan?"

He stood up so suddenly that it startled her. He walked over to the bureau, yanked open the drawers and fumbled through them. Over his shoulder he said, "It's a hell of a life, having to do this sort of thing. Don't look so indignant." He looked in her purse and then looked at the green dress. "Guess you couldn't hide anything under that, Miss Perez." She was conscious of the knife she had taped back to her ribs before dressing.

He sat down again. He yawned and said, "Well, it's like this. About three o'clock today, as near as the guy from the Medical Examiner's office can make it, somebody did a little work on a couple people named Darron and Dziemansek. I understand you know 'em."

Her throat felt dry and tight. It would be dangerous to lie and dangerous not to lie. In a subdued tone she said, "I know them."

"Glad you didn't lie. You wouldn't know 'em now."

Latmini fought for control when the room swam before her eyes. Harrigan's face seemed to swell to five times life size and then recede so far away that she could barely see it. Out of a mist he said, "Sorry I gave it to you so fast. Want some water?"

She nodded and with surprising speed he appeared with a glass of cold water. She sipped it gratefully.

Harrigan said, "I just spent quite a bit of time proving to myself that you didn't leave the hotel after you came back at one thirty-five. Near the phone in the apartment where they were killed is a scratch pad. There was nothing written on it, but on the sheet that was gone somebody had written 'Janice Walters—Arnot.' And here you are. Other people are checking other things. I'm checking you. Okay?" She nodded. "So tell me why your name is on the pad."

"I didn't know where to go for a room. Mr. Roger Darron was supposed to have made a reservation for me. I believe a friend wrote him from Ceylon. I called him when I got in town and he sent me here."

"Also I find out that this Darron, or somebody who looks like he used to look, came to see you."

"He was being friendly. He wondered if I wanted anything."

"Then his gal friend comes to see you at three in the morning. Why?"

"She was jealous. She thought he liked me."

Harrigan grinned at her. She suddenly felt that there was a brain behind those brown eyes, a brain not as naïve as his expresion. And not as friendly. "I can see how you might make her jealous. She didn't look so good when I saw her. What are you doing in this country, Miss Perez?"

"Just a visit. Some shopping. I'm a tourist."

"Who was this friend who steered you to this Darron guy?"

At that moment the phone rang. She hurried to it and pressed the receiver close to her ear so that the sound of Karl's voice wouldn't be audible to the listening Harrigan.

"Stella? I'm down in the bar. Shall I come up?"

"I don't think so. I'd rather not go, if you don't mind. I'm afraid it would be too crowded there."

Karl was quick. "I see," he said softly. "Someone is with you. If you do not need help, say good-by immediately. I will not want to see you tonight, at any rate."

"Good-by," she said and hung up, turning calmly to face Harrigan. He sat and watched her with an amused look in his brown eyes.

For a moment she was afraid that he would ask what place it was that would be too crowded for her tastes. Instead he said, "I was asking you who it was that steered you to this Darron."

"Oh, that was an old friend of my family's. A man named Sakna Kahn, He owns several businesses in Ceylon. He travels quite a bit."

"I see. What about this Wanda Dziemansek? What information can you give us about her?"

"I never saw her or heard of her until she came to my room early this morning. She threatened me if I—became friendly with Mr. Darron. She happened to say that Mr. Darron took her out of a D. P. camp near Munich."

"I wouldn't be surprised if she was in this country illegally. You know, this guy Darron lived pretty well without a job and without much dough. We can't find a sign of a bankbook or a job."

She shrugged as if it was of no interest to her.

But the strain of being calm was beginning to tell. She could feel a small muscle in her upper lip begin to twitch. To her great relief, Harrigan stood up and settled his hat firmly on his head.

He walked leisurely to the door. "Well, we'll keep checking back, Miss Perez. We'll be around when we turn up something."

CHAPTER THREE

Secret in Blood

WHEN the door closed behind him she began to tremble so badly that she could hardly stand. It was pure horror to think that what she had said to Karl about Darron had resulted in— That couldn't be true! It must have been some other enemy. Bad luck. Pure bad luck. With the police in on it, Karl Ehrlich would become cautious and refuse to deal with her. Darron was the only one who knew the method for quick communication with Sakna Kahn. If Sakna Kahn should hear that Darron was dead and that Karl Ehrlich had refused to deal with her—

She stood, still trembling, and tightened her hands until the finger nails bit into her palms. She suddenly realized that Karl would not call again, that Karl would probably never call again. She remembered his air of caution. The unreality of the situation was a constant nightmare. Because one power-mad man in Ceylon saw the British leave India, he wanted to hurry them out of Ceylon. The British garrison was small. It would succeed. For a time. There would be many deaths.

When you dealt in death, you had to deal with men like Ehrlich, Darron and Sakna Kahn. You had to wear a variety of names and when success was in your grasp, you ended up standing in your hotel room, shaking from head to foot. There was a bitter taste in your mouth. You stood and thought of the men who would be sent by Sakna Kahn to the plantation after your two sisters if Sakna Kahn ever suspected the least trace of disloyalty to his blood-stained cause.

She suddenly realized that her only way out would be to see Karl Ehrlich alone. In a place where he would be forced to talk to her. His room! She would have to find a way to get into the room. Finding out which room was easy. She merely phoned the desk and asked and they told her.

She paced back and forth, trying to think of some way to get into his room. Suddenly she grinned crookedly at her own stupidity. It would be easy to find out if he was in there. Room nine twenty-six. One floor above. She found the fire well and went quickly up the stairs. She knocked at his door. No answer. Again. He was not in.

A maid came down the hall, clean sheets over her arm, and went into the room across the hall from nine twenty-six. She used a pass key on the door.

Latmini dipped hurriedly into her purse, found a ten dollar bill, pushed the half-open door wide open and walked in.

'Yeah?" the maid said expectantly, eyeing the ten.

"I wonder if you'd let me in the room across the hall."

"Against the rules. Can't do it."

"But I'm a guest in the hotel. You see, a friend of mine has that room. I want to play a joke on him. Really, I'm not a thief."

"Ask the desk."

"You know they'll say no. Look, I'll make it fifteen dollars."

The maid scratched her thin blonde hair. "Well—"

*   *   *

The room wasn't built for walking. Square and plain, with drab plaster walls, draperies fresh from the showroom of your cheap local dealer in furniture which makes your home look like "the home of the movie stars."

And yet she walked. Ceaselessly. From the bed to the bathroom door. Back. The wide windows looked down on the heart of the city. She felt the deep pulse of the city and it was something that was part of the beat of her heart, something that took possession of nerve, vein, pulse. . . .

There would be no point in calling the desk.

As soon as Karl came back from the meeting, or wherever he was, he would come to the room. There was nothing else he *could* do. It was his room. Karl seemed to be a creature of habit.

She paused, near the windows, held her hands outstretched, fingers spread, felt the excited surge of pulse that made her hands tremble, made a vein throb in her throat, made her feel once again the deep fear that had been with her ever since she had walked up the gangplank at Colombo.

On impulse, she hurried to the bureau, pulled open the drawers, riffling impatiently through the neatly folded underthings, the starched shirts. It was in the second drawer. A plain silver flask bearing the odd seal that she had learned to recognize. Just a plain silver flask, dull finish, inscribed with a warning that she could interpret.

She unscrewed the top, tilted it high and the sharp sting of the liquor tore at her throat. Of course it was good and expensive liquor. Karl would insist on nothing less. The deep rich glow warmed the chill of fear, made her strong again. . . and bold.

It was at the instant that she heard his key in the door. The knob turned. She stood waiting for him, his silver flask in her hand.

He was startled at the glow of light in the room. She saw him blink against the glare, pause, iron out the expression of dismay.

His tone was most casual. "Hello, Stella." As though finding a woman in his room was a customary thing.

She heard, in her own voice, the thin fragile note of hysteria. "Karl!" she said. "How nice! Welcome home."

Without taking his eyes from her, he closed the door behind him. The click of the brass latch was thin, metallic, final, somehow ominous. Karl had become a stranger. Without warning. Without plan.

He walked toward her, stopped three feet away and said, "It is nice, isn't it?" His eyes were cold. "I saw Roger this evening. He told me—just enough."

She backed away suddenly as he reached for her. She couldn't evade the square tanned hand that reached for her throat, but tore the fabric of her dres.

Holding the dark green dress together, she backed against the bed, looking at him with wide eyes.

"I think we will talk this over," he said. He walked slowly toward her.

The flask dropped to the floor. She shrank back.

He paused and smiled. "Or perhaps you would perfer to finish your drink?"

"What do you mean?" she asked, hysteria close to the surface. "Why are you like this?"

He stooped and picked up the flask. Some of the contents had seeped out onto the pale rug. He glanced down at the dark wet spot. She looked also, saw the threads in the rug twist and blacken, saw the tiny wisps of gray smoke that arose, smelled the pungent odor of acid. She put both hands to her throat.

Karl laughed at her. The sound was flat, metallic—somehow reminding her of the click of the door latch. "Don't fret, Stella. This toy is a thing I have seen before. It is the impact which releases the capsule of acid into the liquor. A pretty seal etched into the silver, don't you think? Don't you remember seeing it before?"

She could make no sense of his words. She felt as though she had been pushed onto a stage in an unfamiliar part. The other actor was giving her the cues, but she couldn't respond. "No, I—"

"Think, my clever little one: Think hard! Surely one like you who comes to Karl Ehrlich and pretends to be a customer must also be observant."

"I did not pretend. I have—"

His voice softened. "My dear, a man does not lie when he looks into the eyes of death. Roger Darron labeled you an imposter when he said that you have nothing of value with you."

HIS huge frame and the uncanny quickness of his movements made any thought of escape impossible. She lifted her chin, tried to make her voice firm and confident. "But surely Roger Darron told you more than that. He must have—"

"Stella, my sweet, he had no chance to say more."

"Then you—"

The slience in the room was intense. Her mouth dry, she looked into his eyes and saw what Roger Daron had seen—and Wanda. She saw the way Wanda had walked back and forth, suddenly alive as she talked of Roger. She saw Roger's vague blue eyes, his florid face, the red puffiness of his hands. A fragment of memory returned. There had been a ring on the third finger of his left hand. A heavy ring, the flesh bulging above and below it. An odd seal on that ring. The seal matched the design on the flask.

Inadvertently she said, "His ring."

"I knew you were observant, Stella. Now you know far too much, don't you? When he was blinded he fumbled for that flask. I thought it must be some sort of a key to his activities. I brought it back here with me and put it away in the drawer. You must be psychic, my dear. Something led you directly to it. Now, suppose you tell me, very quickly, who your represent, what you are after."

He stepped closer to her, one of his big hands clamping on her wrist. He twisted slightly, and the pain shot through her arm.

"Who sent you to me?" he asked, accenting each word.

He had his right hand on her left wrist. She moved a bit closer to him, and smiled. She slipped her right hand through the tear in her dress, snatched the jade hilt of the knife, felt the tape pull away from her flesh. She snapped it down to fling off the sheath and then drove it up at him.

He twisted back. The keen blade slit the fabric of his suit and that was all.

"The kitten has claws," he said softly. On his toes, like a boxer, he began to move cautiously toward her. "It will be better if it is your knife that is used," he said.

The door broke open with a splintering crash and Harrigan bounded into the room, the light glinting on the steady muzzle of the revolver he held aimed at Ehrlich's middle. "Break it off right here, kids," he said softly.

Ehrlich snatched the knife by the blade, pulling the hilt out of Latmini's lax hand. With the same sweeping motion, he threw it at Harrigan, bounding after it like a great cat.

The crash of the shot in the small room was like the crack of a thousand whips. Harrigan had fired as he jumped back. He stood, his back against the closet door, and the jade handle of the knife quivered close to his head. His rush caried Karl heavily into the wall near the door. Then Karl crashed to the floor and lay still.

Harigan put one toe under Ehrlich's shoulder and grunted as he kicked him over. "Oh, unhappy day!" Harrigan said. "Right smack in the face. And so many people wanted to have words with him."

He kicked the shattered door shut in the face of a shaking man who stood there, his eyes bulging. He said to Latmini, "Sit down, honey. I got a call to make."

She sat numbly on the bed. It was finished now. Sakna Kahn would believe that he had been betrayed. Anything he might do, he would consider as a lesson to others who would think of betrayal.

She heard the murmur of Harrigan's voice as he spoke over the phone. He hung up.

"What made you come here?" she asked in a low voice.

"We've had this outfit covered like a tent, sweetness. Our man was on the switchboard when I was in your room. One of the Federal agencies has been fastened to Ehrlich like a leech for months. We coordinated a little. That reminds me." He stepped out into the hall, pushed some people aside and picked up a stethoscope from the floor, came back into the room and kicked the door shut.

"A very old gag, honey, but a good one. He was too smart for the boys to plant wires on. So I got this in a hurry from a doc in the hotel. Flat against the door, you can hear pretty good."

She stared over at the dead face of Karl Ehrlich and shuddered.

"What's the matter, honey?" Harrison asked. "You've heard about these things. The boys will be along in a few minutes now to wrap up Ehrlich. You'll have to answer our questions, then we turn you over to the Federal boys for a thorough going over."

"It won't do any good," she said dully. "It has all gone wrong for me. Everything. Nothing will do any good now."

He walked over to her, squatted on his heels in front of her and peered up into her face. "Maybe you should tell Harrigan," he said softly. "You sound beat."

"I'll tell you, but it won't do any good. I was sent here to contact this man and buy weapons for shipment to Ceylon. I have failed. The man who sent me here will take his revenge on my family."

Harrigan frowned. "So that's why Ehrlich here was such an interesting item

to the boys from Washington! But have you got that kind of money on you?"

She silently shook her head.

He stood up. "Then Harrigan can't do anything for you, honey. We need a little more than a fairy tale from a beautiful lady to swing us into action."

She shrugged hopelessly. "What could you do?"

"Simple. Our British cousins are also interested in Ehrlich, even though he's dead. I spent some time in CIC during the late fracas. I know how far they'll play along. With proof of some kind from you, I'll bet they'd send their people to your family, pick them up and hold them in protective custody."

Slowly she lifted her head. "Do you mean it? Really?"

"Of course I mean it."

She stood up and wavered weakly. He caught her by the elbows and said, "Steady as she goes, lass." For a moment their eyes met. She felt that something had passed between them. A certain understanding. With an odd flash of prescience, she knew that this man would be mixed up in all the rest of her life.

She walked to the closet door and said, as she wrenched the knife out of the wood, "You said there is a doctor in the hotel. Call him immediately."

He stared at the knife. "But what—"

"Call him!"

As he crossed to the phone she went over and sat on the bed. He replaced the phone on the cradle and said, "He'll come running. Now what—"

She had pulled the skirt of the green dress up above her knees. She glanced at Harrigan. He licked dry lips and she saw the confusion in his eyes.

Her mouth twisted into a grimace of anticipated pain, and she placed the keen edge of the blade against the ridge of white scar tissue, pressed down and drew the blade quickly across the scar, biting deep. The dark blood flowed quickly. Faint with pain, she flexed her thigh to bunch the muscles, pressed hard with her thumbs on either side of the wound.

A dark object slipped from the wound and thudded against the rug. She tried to press again, but all strength had gone from her fingers. Weakly she said to Harrigan, "Emerald . . . nearly thirty karat . . . imbedded in tissue . . . sterile . . . two others still there . . . half-million dollars . . . they were stolen from Buddhist temple."

She felt herself going over forward and tried to catch her balance, but it was too late. As the room darkened, she knew that Harrigan took a quick step and caught her. A strange voice asked something about a patient. She couldn't hear it clearly because Harrigan's arms were around her, and his voice, deep and gentle, was saying, "It will be all right. Don't be afraid. It will be all right."

THE END

(Continued from page 51)

She stopped me. "Wait a minute, honey. If you're goin' after him again, forget it. You'll never get him. No woman will. I—I don't know. I ain't very good with words, but it seems to me Max—he may pick up with a woman for a little while, but he'll always go back to his first sweetie—that dam' horn, that dam' music. Believe me, honey. Forget him."

Maybe I could forget him. Maybe I couldn't. But I had to find Max Mercer. We had a date with Ina Courtney—that cold-blooded little tramp wasn't getting away with murder.

I started to say something to Diana about Max Mercer, but what was there to say? Outside, going down that crumby stairway, way inside of me, I knew Diana was right. The only part of Max Mercer any woman would *really* have would be his music.

THE END

(Continued from page 29)

bodies, Spence, down there around St. Lo—"

"No!"

It was a scream of madness, tearing through the Long Bar. Heads turned to watch Spencer Grail, standing there, shivering, his thin face working convulsively. "No, no, no, no!"

And then he turned and stumbled out the door, muttering incoherently, like an animal, the sweat running down his face.

"Dammit, Bruce!" I exploded. "What in the hell is the matter with you?"

Bruce was shaken, too, but he still had the power of action in his body. He got up quickly and pushed away from the booth. He muttered, "I'll go get him, Mort. I'll bring him back. . . ."

And with that (I told the lieutenant) he went after Spencer.

* * *

It was quiet in the little police car, when the monotonous chant which had been my voice died away. The lieutenant's pencil stopped scratching, and he put the book and the pencil away with what seemed particular carefulness.

He turned his head slightly, so that he looked past me, out the car window, toward the knot of people a short distance away.

"The one the beat cop had to shoot?" he asked.

I licked my lips. "That—that was Spencer Grail," I said.

"And the fellow he'd been kneeling on, the one with the broken neck and the torn-up body. . . . That was Bruce Carter?"

"Yes." I shuddered. "That was Bruce."

"The wise guy?" the lieutenant said.

"The wise guy," I said.